BOOK I

SUZANNAH
AND THE
SECRET COINS

ELAINE SCHULTE

BJU PRESS
Greenville, South Carolina

Library of Congress Cataloging-in-Publication Data
Schulte, Elaine L.
    Suzannah and the secret coins / Elaine Schulte.
        p. cm. — (A Colton cousins adventure ; bk. 1)
    Summary: In 1848 twelve-year-old Suzannah and her cousin
Daniel travel with their families from the East Coast along the
National Road, also known as the Cumberland Road, to the Missouri
frontier, and a blizzard, bear chase, and other dangers along the way
make them glad to have God's strength on their side.
    ISBN 1-57924-563-3 (alk. paper)
    [1. Frontier and pioneer life—Fiction. 2. Cousins—Fiction. 3.
Cumberland Road—Fiction. 4. Christian life—Fiction.] I. Title.

PZ7.S3867 Su 2001
[Fic]—dc21   00-140186

Suzannah and the Secret Coins

Elaine L. Schulte

Designed by Brannon McAllister
Cover and illustrations by Johanna Berg Ehnis

© 1992 Elaine Schulte
© 2001 Bob Jones University Press
Greenville, SC 29614

ISBN 1-57924-563-3

15 14 13 12 11 10 9 8 7 6 5 4 3 2 1

*To the Shining Lights on the hill
at SFC in Solana Beach*

Contents

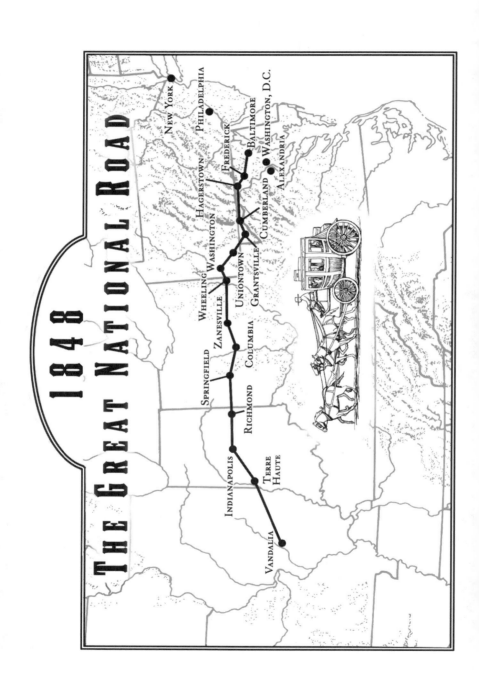

1848
The Great National Road

New York
Philadelphia
Hagerstown
Frederick
Baltimore
Washington, D.C.
Cumberland
Alexandria
Wheeling
Washington
Uniontown
Grantsville
Zanesville
Columbia
Springfield
Richmond
Indianapolis
Terre Haute
Vandalia

CHAPTER 1

"Pack up! Pack up! We're moving West!"

Twelve-year-old Suzannah Colton rose from the parlor armchair, and the sock she'd been darning fell from her lap.

"Hurry!" called her brother-in-law, slamming the front door behind him. "We're leaving at midnight!"

At midnight? Suzannah's mind echoed.

Angry voices buzzed in the entry hall.

Moments later her sister, Pauline, stepped into the parlor, her face as pale as rice powder. She threw Suzannah a worried glance, then turned to her husband, her chin quivering. "You'll have to explain to Suzannah, too, Charles."

"We're moving to Missouri, and we're leaving tonight." Charles stared down at her, his eyes an icy black.

"Missouri?" Suzannah gasped. "You mean . . . the frontier?"

"Aren't you the one who told your cousin Daniel you wished you could go with them?"

"Well, yes . . . but I thought it was impossible—"

"It has suddenly *become* possible." He smiled, but the smile did not reach his eyes. "I've arranged for us to travel together."

"Charles, please . . . won't you reconsider?" Pauline broke in. "Suzannah and I grew up in Alexandria. All our friends live here—"

"The house and furnishings have already been sold," Charles interrupted. "Now hurry!"

Suzannah cried out, "Father's house . . . sold? But why?"

Her brother-in-law avoided her eyes. "That's not for little girls to ask."

Suzannah bristled. That's how Charles *always* side-stepped an argument. Well, she was not a little girl any longer! Sometimes she even felt older than Pauline. She faced him, blazing with anger.

"You gambled it away, didn't you? It wasn't enough that you lost your own parents' home in a card game! You had to go and—"

"Never mind that!" He cut her short. "The house is sold, and we're leaving tonight. Now, upstairs, both of you. A carriage will be here at midnight, and we'll be in it, with or without your things. I'll get the trunks." He brushed past them and headed up the steps to the attic.

Suzannah felt like a balloon with the air let out.

"I'm so sorry—" Pauline began.

Suzannah knew her sister was sorry about more than leaving Virginia. She was sorry she'd ever married Charles Herrington.

"He means it," her sister said. "We'd better pack now, or we'll have only the clothes on our backs."

Suzannah ran up the stairs ahead of Pauline, her long, thick braids flying. It wasn't as if they were going alone, she reminded herself. Cousin Daniel, who was almost thirteen, and his parents would be going too. And it *was* 1848. The National Road went clear to Vandalia, Illinois now.

At the top of the staircase, she lit a candle. "Maybe it will turn out to be an exciting adventure," she said, trying to make her sister feel better.

"Maybe." Pauline looked older than her twenty-one years. "Still, to flee like thieves in the night . . . take you from school. I never meant to drag you into all of this." She made a helpless gesture. "I thought—"

Suzannah knew what Pauline was thinking as they went into their bedrooms. Charles had seemed so pleasant during their courtship—mature and quite dashing and rich! Why, before they married, he couldn't do enough for Pauline. He'd treated her like a queen—and Suzannah, too, bringing her little treats tucked into the bouquets he'd given to her older sister.

But things changed soon after Father and Mother died. For one thing, Pauline panicked. "What will become of us?" she asked Suzannah after the double funeral. "We can't take care of ourselves. I'm eighteen . . . old enough to be married, even if I haven't known Charles very long—"

But no matter how much Suzannah tried to convince her sister that they could manage alone, Pauline didn't rest until a gold band was safely on her finger. She had married Charles Herrington within a month after the funeral.

In her bedroom, Suzannah put the flickering candle on the chest of drawers, pulled out warm clothing from the clothes cupboard, and piled it on her bed. Next she got out Mother's small brown traveling bag. Dear Mother. What would she think if she could see them now? She would probably fret as much over the unknown dangers of the frontier—savage Indians, wild animals—as over the loss of her house because of Charles's gambling habit. But even if she were here, there wasn't anything Mother could do about it. There wasn't anything *anyone* could do.

Suddenly Suzannah remembered. Maybe there was something she could do—

Going to the bedroom door, Suzannah glanced down the empty hallway. Hurrying back inside, she crouched by her bed and thrust her arm deep under the mattress. Feeling the leather pouch, she pulled it out. At least Charles hadn't gotten his hands on *this!* She tucked the pouch into a corner of her mother's old travel bag, burying it under everything else. The long drawstrings of the bag would fit around her neck so she could wear it hidden under her cloak.

What else should she take? A framed daguerreotype of her parents, the sampler she had cross-stitched when she was ten, an old doll. She gathered mementos, then thought of her change purse. She'd carry it on top in the traveling bag. Then, if robbers came upon them, she'd just hand them the purse—

Charles huffed into the room and dropped a heavy trunk beside her bed. "No time for daydreaming!"

"I'll be ready!" she snapped to keep from crying and began to fill the trunk as fast as she could.

"Wake up, Suzannah! Wake up! Hurry!"

Suzannah felt a hand on her shoulder. Groaning, she opened her eyes.

Her sister stood over her bed, a candle trembling in her hand. "Time to leave. The driver is here for the trunks. It's well after midnight already—"

Suzannah squinted into the candlelight. "Are we really going?"

"Yes. I have to get Jamie up. Charles has ridden ahead."

At this Suzannah sat bolt upright. "Charles . . . gone?"

"He'll meet us later. Hurry!" Pauline rushed from the room.

Instantly alert, Suzannah climbed out of bed. Her trunk stood open, and a dark blue traveling dress hung over a chair. She dressed quickly, then threw her nightgown into the trunk and locked it.

Just in time, too, for the pudding-faced driver clumped into her room without so much as asking permission. "This bag goin'?"

Suzannah whirled around and grabbed her mother's traveling bag. "I'll carry it myself, thank you!"

He shrugged, then hoisted the trunk to his shoulder. "Up to you. Hurry now. Got my orders."

Suzannah tightened the drawstrings of the traveling bag, then pulled on her dark blue hooded cloak and followed the driver down the stairs. Pauline trailed behind, carrying Jamie, who slept on her shoulder. As they moved through the house, they snuffed out the candles.

"Suzannah, can you carry the food?" Pauline whispered so as not to wake Jamie. "We'll have to eat in the carriage."

Suzannah lifted the wicker basket from the kitchen table, then blew out the last candle. The house was as dark and empty as her heart felt.

Outside, a full moon shone through the trees, casting eerie shadows and turning the bare branches into gnarled fingers, clawing the night sky. A cold wind blew, sending a few dry leaves scampering across the lawn before swirling into the air. Though it was late February, winter was far from over, and the air held a hint of snow. Suzannah shivered and noticed that Pauline tucked the blanket more securely around Jamie who whimpered as he stirred in his sleep.

"Shhh," the driver shushed loudly, leading them out the back way to the shed. "Keep that babe quiet."

"Hush, darlin'. Hush now." Pauline comforted Jamie, rocking him back to sleep.

Silently they climbed into the waiting carriage. Before they could settle themselves, the carriage lurched forward, and they fell back into their seats.

Suzannah sat up, untangled her cloak and skirts, and pulled back the curtain for one last look at the brick house, bathed in moonlight. "Oh, Pauline—"

"I know . . . oh, I know—"

As the horses clip-clopped down the familiar street, her whole lifetime—all twelve years—flashed before Suzannah's eyes. Right next door was her best friend's house, as dark as the rest. Would she ever see Jenny again? And two streets down, she could see the steeple of the church where Mother had insisted that they never miss a Sunday.

Suzannah clutched her traveling bag more tightly.

They heard the crack of the driver's whip, then the carriage picked up speed. Faster and faster they went, clattering wildly over the cobblestone streets.

"Why are we going so fast?"

"I don't know!" Pauline clutched the baby with one hand and the side strap with the other. "See if you can get the driver to slow down."

Suzannah poked her head out the window. Then she heard it—hoofbeats! Horses galloping hard after them! In the distance she could make out the shape of a second carriage. It was gaining on them.

"Hold on!" she yelled. "Someone's after us!"

"Oh, Suzannah, pray!"

But Suzannah couldn't find the words to pray. She held onto her traveling bag. What if it were stolen? What would they do then?

Desperately she and her sister clung to the passenger straps. Jamie woke and began to cry, adding his wails to the sounds of the carriage in hot pursuit.

Just at that moment, shots rang out, and Pauline screamed.

"Whoa, boys, whoa!" the driver shouted, reining in the terror-stricken horses.

A stream of profanity filled the crisp night air. Suddenly the carriage door was jerked open, and a lantern was thrust into the interior. A man's hawk-nosed face, fierce in the dim glow of light, followed.

"Where's Charles Herrington?" he demanded.

Pauline's eyes widened. Her arms tightened protectively around Jamie, and he began to cry.

"Shut that brat up before he wakes the countryside!" the man growled, looking nervously over his shoulder.

"Hush, Jamie." Pauline put her hand over his mouth to smother his cries. "Please hush!"

"Where's Herrington, I say?"

"I told you. He ain't here," said the driver, jumping down from his perch. "Ain't supposed to say, but he rode on to Baltimore to book passage on a ship around the Horn."

The man scowled at Suzannah. "That true?"

She glared back at him from her corner. It would be just like Charles to tell them one thing, then do another.

Impatient, the man grabbed her shoulder and shook her. "Answer me!"

She pulled away. "Don't you touch me!"

"Girl, you better tell what you know!"

"But we *don't* know," Pauline said, leaning forward timidly. "Please, you have to believe us."

"You better not be lying!" The hawk-nosed man shook his fist at them and gave Suzannah another menacing frown before he withdrew the lantern and rushed into the night.

The driver stood gazing into the darkness after their assailants. "Ain't they got some nerve?" he said, sounding far braver now that the carriage had disappeared around a bend in the road. "Guess we've seen the last of them. We'd best be off."

Suzannah didn't feel any too sure of it as she sat back against the cold seat. What would keep those men from following them to find Charles?

Once the excitement had died down and they were under way, Pauline and Jamie fell into an exhausted sleep.

Suzannah laid her head back and glanced at Pauline. Her sister took after their mother, as thin and easily shaken as a willow tree. She slept now with her blond head drooping over Jamie.

Pauline had always been the pretty one—all dimples and golden curls and pale skin—while she herself had been the spunky one. "You've got gumption, Suzannah," Father had said. "You're not apt to lose your head when there's trouble." Well, this was trouble, sure enough. She only hoped Father was right.

She glanced again at Pauline to make sure she was asleep, then reached into her travel bag and pulled out the small pouch he had given her several months before he died. She opened it and poured its contents into her lap.

"One, two, three—" Suzannah counted out the large gold coins, then the medium-sized and smaller ones.

As she returned the coins to the pouch and stuffed them into her bag, she remembered what Father had said when he gave them to her: "You may need these someday, Suzannah. Don't spend them unless it's absolutely necessary, and don't tell anyone about them, not even your sister. Keep them well hidden—"

Suzannah sighed and leaned back against her seat. Having the coins was almost like having Father near with his gentle wisdom and strength. They might have plenty of trouble in the journey ahead, but as long as she had the gold coins, they would be safe.

CHAPTER 2

The first pink rays of dawn were curving over the earth toward Washington City when Suzannah awoke, surprised that she had slept. She sat up in the carriage, her back stiff.

In the first light, the stately new buildings of the nation's capital gleamed white and new—the domed Capitol, the President's White Mansion, the Treasury Building, and the Patent Office, where Father had worked with inventors. At the sight of the Patent Office, Suzannah's heart knotted with grief. If Father hadn't worked there on new inventions, he and Mother would never have been killed in that awful steamboat explosion on the Potomac River.

She tried to forget and looked at the city itself. It seemed more grand than usual. For one thing, it was too early for laundry to be flapping from hotel clotheslines. And no pigs foraged for food in the streets yet.

The carriage drew up in front of John Coleman's Hotel, the finest in Washington City. Their driver climbed down and, smoothing his rumpled clothing, headed for the front entrance.

Pauline awoke, and Jamie untangled himself from his favorite yellow blanket and sat, yawning, between them.

"Is this where we'll be staying?" Suzannah asked.

"I think so. Charles had business with some men at this hotel," Pauline explained. "The driver is to make arrangements."

Moments later, however, their driver ran out, chased by two angry men in their nightshirts. "Don't you or Charles Herrington ever show yerselves here again!"

"Oh, dear—" Pauline whispered. "I guess we won't be staying here, after all."

The driver leaped onto the carriage box, called out to the horses, and they rolled on down the street.

Jamie, frightened by the loud voices, cried out, and Pauline picked him up and held him close. "Don't cry, Jamie, please don't cry. Papa promised to take care of everything. He *promised*—"

Suzannah smoothed the folds of her blue cloak. She wasn't so sure her brother-in-law would take care of anything. Maybe they would never even see him again.

Jouncing along the Washington Pike, there was nothing to do but eat the buttered cornbread and apples Pauline had packed. They had saved some for lunch and were glad to have it as they rode through Maryland's wintry countryside.

"The sights are pleasant enough," Pauline said. She had brought along a new sketchbook and, opening it, began to sketch the passing scenes while Jamie slept.

Suzannah nodded. It calmed her to watch her sister work. Pauline always caught her lower lip between her teeth as she sketched. She drew things that Suzannah never noticed, like a bird sitting on the split rail fence, his head cocked as if wondering why the humans didn't fly too.

After a while she interrupted the silence. "Tell me about Aunt Pearl in Independence, Missouri."

Pauline shrugged. "Uncle Franklin says she's almost as nice as Aunt Ruthie, and Aunt Ruthie says her sister is nicer."

"*That's* hard to believe."

Pauline nodded. "She's younger than Aunt Ruthie, and since her husband and two children died of the fever last year, she's lonely and glad for Aunt Ruthie's family to come."

"Sure hope *we're* welcome," Suzannah said.

"We'll find a house there as soon as we can," Pauline promised. "Charles won't want to live with another family."

Night had fallen by the time they arrived in the small town of Frederick. The driver halted the horses in front of the City Hotel. He opened the carriage door for them. "Well, here you are," he said before unloading their trunks and carrying them to the hotel. "Hope you have a safe ride to Baltimore."

Pauline thanked him and bade him farewell.

When he'd left, Suzannah blurted, "Baltimore?"

"Never mind," her sister replied. "Just come along." Pauline led the way to the innkeeper's desk. She told him, "Our driver made a mistake. Please get us another carriage so that we can travel on."

"Some carriages right outside," the innkeeper replied.

Suddenly Suzannah understood. "This is Charles's doing, isn't it?" she asked once they were alone.

Pauline pressed her lips together, and tears welled in her eyes. "I'm only doing what he told me to if the plan to stay in Washington City fell through."

"Oh, Pauline—" Suzannah wished she could be comforting, but it was just as awful to switch hotels as it had been to leave home like thieves in the night. Probably for the same reason, too—Charles wanting to throw those men off his trail.

At length, they were packed, bag and baggage, into another carriage, and ten minutes later, deposited at the Frederick Hotel.

"What now?" Suzannah asked.

Pauline bundled up Jamie who was asleep. "I—I expect Charles will be here soon."

When the driver returned to collect their fare, however, Pauline's mouth dropped open in shock. "But I don't have that much money. . . . My husband said it would be much less. This is all I have—"

The man grabbed the money from Pauline's hand. "With me carryin' those heavy trunks? Nosiree! I'll hold yer baggage here. I don't aim to be fleeced!"

Suzannah clutched her brown bag more tightly under her arm. She couldn't spend the gold coins at the very beginning of the journey. She just couldn't.

Pauline turned to the desk clerk. "Has Mr. Charles Herrington checked in?"

The man ran a finger down the guest list, then peered at her over large gold spectacles. "We don't have reservations for anyone by that name."

Pauline and Suzannah stared at each other in dismay.

"Do you have any Coltons staying here?"

The man brightened. "We're expecting a Mr. and Mrs. Franklin Colton and son, Daniel, from Georgetown."

Suzannah let out her breath. *Aunt Ruthie, Uncle Franklin, and Cousin Daniel!*

The desk clerk added, "They're headed west, I believe. A good many folk gather here to catch the stagecoaches on the National Road . . . or the Cumberland Road, as some call it."

Suzannah nodded, trying to hide her relief. . . .

She turned to Pauline and saw that Jamie was still asleep in her sister's arms. "Let's wait in the lobby and watch for them. And think how to get our baggage back from that driver too."

Just as they started toward some inviting chairs in the lobby, the door opened and there stood Daniel, their almost-thirteen-year-old cousin. Freckles, cowlick and all, he looked like a knight in a rumpled brown homespun suit!

"Daniel!" Suzannah called out.

"Suzannah!" He came toward her. "What's the trouble?"

Suzannah explained their dilemma, holding on tightly to the brown travel bag.

"He wants *more* money?" Daniel repeated, his green eyes wide. He looked in the direction of the driver, who was beginning to slink toward the nearest exit.

Daniel squared his shoulders and followed him. "For what you've been paid, the least you can do is carry my cousins' baggage to the desk."

The man started to leave, but Uncle Franklin's wide-shouldered frame filled the doorway behind him, barring the way. His freckled face was usually kindness itself, but now it was wearing a frown. "Some kind of trouble here?"

The man shook his head. "No—no . . . ain't no trouble a'tall. I was jest restin' me back and gettin' ready to carry in yer family's baggage."

"Good," Uncle Franklin said. "You do that. You look like a man who wouldn't take advantage of two women traveling alone. Let me hold the door open for you."

"Yessir," the driver said and rushed out.

"Well," Uncle Franklin said, "that's that." He grinned—not just a smile that lifted the corners of his mouth, but a big wide grin that reminded Suzannah of Father.

Aunt Ruthie, who was as short as Uncle Franklin was tall, shook her head, but her dimples and blue eyes danced with laughter. "That's your uncle for you, turning troublesome folk into possibilities."

"Like Father did," Suzannah said.

"Exactly," her aunt replied and caught Suzannah in her arms. She gave her a good hug, then stood back. "We're so glad you and Pauline and Jamie are going with us to Missouri."

Suzannah decided not to spoil the moment. There would be plenty of time later to ask about Charles . . . and to tell of the mysterious man who had stopped their carriage last night . . . and of the men who had chased the driver from the hotel in Washington City in their nightshirts . . . not to mention changing hotels!

"You girls must be exhausted," Aunt Ruthie said, "jouncing up and down in that carriage since the middle of the night!"

"We've put in quite a day ourselves, what with closing out our shop and shipping goods for a new trading post in Missouri," Uncle Franklin said. "We sent off three

Conestoga freight wagons full. Daniel did more than his share of the packing, I can tell you." He beamed fondly at his son.

Daniel grinned back, but Suzannah thought his face seemed a little pale under his freckles.

Still, tired as they were, Daniel Meriwether Colton and Uncle Franklin Meriwether Colton glowed with excitement. They'd been middle-named for Meriwether Lewis, the great explorer of the Oregon Territory, which Aunt Ruthie claimed "gave them feet that just itched for adventure." Now, at long last, they would have it.

Uncle Franklin patted Suzannah's shoulder. "We can hear all about your trip tomorrow at breakfast."

Tomorrow morning was soon enough, Suzannah decided. Besides, with Uncle Franklin at her side, she felt safe. It was almost as good as being with Father.

Before long they were situated in their modest rooms, then in bed. Just as Suzannah drifted off into sleep, something new occurred to her. This might be one time Charles had no intention of paying his gambling debts. Maybe he was taking the money from the sale of their house and furnishings to the frontier. And maybe those men suspected as much. No wonder they were after him!

The next morning, while Pauline dressed Jamie in their room, Suzannah looked at the mementos in her trunk. She picked up the picture of Mother and Father. In it, Mother's golden hair was pulled back into a neat bun. She looked just like Pauline. As for Father . . . well, Suzannah knew she resembled him—freckles, brown hair with a stubborn cowlick, and that famous grin. For an instant she held the picture against her cheek.

"Courage," Father would have said.

And Mother's favorite Psalm came to mind: *Yea, though I walk through the valley of the shadow of death, I will fear no evil: for thou art with me.*

Suzannah blew her bangs up from her forehead and took out her favorite sampler. The alphabet was cross-stitched in bright colors over a house and trees. On the bottom she had embroidered:

Suzannah Colton is my name
America is my nation
Alexandria is my dwelling place
And Christ is my salvation.

If Mother could see down from heaven right now, what would she think of Charles's actions? And what would Father think?

Suzannah knew what she thought. She would never forgive Charles for forcing them to leave Alexandria like this.

"We'd better hurry downstairs for breakfast. Everyone will be waiting," Pauline said.

Suzannah tucked the mementos back into her trunk and locked it, then grabbed her traveling bag. Together they left the room and went downstairs.

To her amazement, Charles himself was waiting in the doorway of the hotel dining room. He wore one of his fine suits, and every dark hair was in place on his handsome head.

"Good morning, my dear." He greeted Pauline as if nothing were amiss.

"Good morning, Charles." Her sister's voice was strained.

He dropped a kiss on her golden hair. "Please forgive yesterday's arrangements. I promise to explain most fully. You'll understand, I assure you."

Pauline nodded.

When Charles looked at Suzannah, she forced out a cold "Good morning."

He gave her a courtly bow. "Now isn't this going to be a grand adventure?"

"You mean sailing around the Horn?" Suzannah asked. "Or going to Missouri?"

He laughed heartily. "I'd think either would be an adventure, especially for a girl who's never traveled farther from Alexandria than Georgetown and Washington City."

"You have no right to—to—"

"I have *every* right to take care of you and my wife and child as I see fit," he interrupted smoothly. "You seem to forget, Suzannah, that you are only twelve years old and that the courts have given me legal control of your life."

"And of *our* money!" she sputtered. "You've lost our house and furniture and everything!"

"Now, now," he soothed, "let's not announce our little differences to the entire hotel."

"Little differences?"

He smiled, but the smile froze on his lips. "Suzannah—" he warned.

Seeing that some of the hotel guests were beginning to stare, she clamped her mouth shut.

"Here, let me carry that travel bag for you," Charles offered, reaching for the strap that hung over her shoulder.

Suzannah pulled it aside. "Don't you touch it!"

Charles gave her a peculiar look. Fortunately, the innkeeper arrived just then and beckoned them into the noisy dining room. "Follow me, please. The rest of your family is already seated."

Pauline obeyed, Jamie toddling at her side. So Suzannah had no choice but to walk in beside Charles.

"Did you have a good journey?" Charles asked. He obviously intended to keep up appearances in spite of the strain between them.

"It wasn't dull," Suzannah said dryly.

"Well, excitement is the spice of life, isn't it?"

"Not *that* kind of excitement! It's a wonder we weren't hurt!"

He lifted his dark brows, but she couldn't very well explain in the middle of the dining room. She'd let Pauline tell him about the carriage chase.

When they arrived at the long table, a shaft of morning sunlight streamed through the window behind her family, giving them all a golden glow. Daniel and Uncle Franklin rose to their feet, looking freshly scrubbed. Anyone would know they were father and son with their green eyes, determined chins, and sandy brown hair with matching cowlicks.

Aunt Ruthie patted a place on the bench beside her. "Come sit between me and Daniel, Suzannah. I can't think of a better way of starting this bright day than having breakfast with you."

Suzannah smiled. Uncle Franklin often called his wife "Ruthie Sunshine." This morning, more than ever, Aunt Ruthie lived up to her name. Her plump form seemed solid and comforting, and her sweet face beamed encouragement. Suzannah sank down beside her.

The table was already covered with platters of steaming cornbread, eggs, bacon, and ham, and the serving girl was making her way around with pots of coffee and hot chocolate.

"May I help you to eggs and some fine Maryland ham, my dear?" Charles asked Pauline as though nothing unusual had happened.

"Yes, thank you, Charles," she replied, surprised. She held out her thick plate as he served her.

Suzannah turned an unbelieving look on Daniel. Daniel leaned over to her and whispered, "He promised Father not to get into more trouble if we let all of you come with us."

"So *that's* it!" Suzannah shot a look at Charles. "Wonder how long he'll keep it up."

"I don't know. But I wouldn't count on it lasting."

From across the table, Uncle Franklin gave her a wink.

She remembered the talks she'd had with him after her parents died and his attempts to help her understand Charles's gambling habit. "Most people start out making a *little* mistake, like lying," Uncle Franklin had said. "They lie a few times, then more and more until their whole lives are caught up in lying. I suppose Charles gambled just a little at first, too, then a little more until he couldn't stop himself. That's how sin takes over, little by little, even when we don't mean for it to."

Their discussion had helped her to understand Charles better, but it had not changed the facts. Charles was still up to his old tricks, as far as she could tell.

As breakfast continued, though, Charles was as good as could be. He even helped Jamie pick raisins out of his toast. And Pauline looked happier than she had in days.

Just as Suzannah was beginning to relax and enjoy her breakfast, the innkeeper came in. "Stagecoach for

Cumberland Gap and beyond leaves in twenty minutes!" he announced.

"That's us," Suzannah said, half-fearful and half-excited.

Charles excused himself from the table. "I'll see to it that everyone's luggage is brought down and loaded."

"How . . . how kind of you, Charles." Pauline seemed a little breathless, Suzannah thought—all starry-eyed and soft, like when she and Charles were courting. Could Pauline possibly believe this act he was putting on now? Sometimes her older sister acted as young and innocent as . . . as Jamie!

"My pleasure," Charles replied and hurried off.

"Hmmph," Suzannah said, not quite under her breath.

"Hmmph," Daniel echoed beside her.

"Wait till you hear about our trip so far," she whispered to him.

While everyone else was talking, she told Daniel about the man who had stopped their carriage, and about the ones running out of the Washington City hotel to look for Charles.

"In their nightshirts?" Daniel asked.

She nodded, and he clapped a hand to his mouth to hide his grin.

"It might sound funny now, but it wasn't then!" Suzannah said. "Besides, who knows what might happen next?"

"Father thinks Charles will settle down now that he's been given a last chance."

"I hope so," Suzannah said. It didn't hurt to look on the bright side of things. Still, it gave her courage to feel the brown traveling bag with the coins in it tucked securely between her feet.

CHAPTER 3

"Last call! Overland stage leaving for the Cumberland Gap and beyond in five minutes!"

"Here we go!" Suzannah said as they all started for the hotel door, pulling on their warm outer clothes.

Outside, a brave sun pushed its way through lead gray clouds, melting the dirty patches of snow. The wind was cold, though, and Suzannah held her blue cloak closed in front of her.

"Hurry!" Charles hustled them toward the bright green Concord stage with the words "Overland Stagecoach" spelled out on the side. The six huge horses hitched to the coach snorted and stamped their feet as if they were as eager as Charles to be off.

"Where are our belongings?" Aunt Ruthie asked.

"Already aboard," Charles assured her, gesturing toward the baggage strapped into the boot on the back of the coach. On top, an iron railing secured the trunks.

"Quickly!" Charles urged. "Everyone inside!"

While the others climbed into the stagecoach, Suzannah hung back with Daniel. "What's Charles up to now? He's as nervous as a wildcat."

Daniel eyed the man with suspicion. "Maybe someone's still after him."

Glancing about the loading area, she noticed that Charles's horse was not among those tied to the post. Nor did she see the stallion being brought from the hotel livery stable with the others.

"Where's Lucky?" she asked Charles when she reached the steps of the stagecoach.

He smiled another one of those icy smiles that froze on his lips. "Don't you worry about a thing. Get in like a good girl so we can be under way."

The tall boy who had helped load the baggage gave her a look that made her skin crawl. The linings of his faded coat were ragged and torn. "Yer holdin' up the stage!" he snapped.

She climbed into the coach without another word.

Inside, Aunt Ruthie, Uncle Franklin, and Pauline, with Jamie on her lap, had taken the back seat. Three older passengers perched awkwardly on the middle bench. A young boy sat alone on the seat that faced backwards, leaving two spaces beside him for Suzannah and Daniel. She supposed Charles would ride on top with the driver so he'd seem important.

She sat down on the crackling cold leather seat by the window. Not that these were real windows, of course. On the rough overland trails, glass would break, so leather curtains covered the window openings to keep out the cold.

Cousin Daniel took the middle seat beside her, and they pulled the buffalo robes up over their laps.

"I'll let you sit by the window whenever you want," she offered.

"Thanks. But I think I'll wait for a better view," he joked. "Indians on the warpath, or something."

Suzannah grinned and gave him an elbow to the ribs, only to be elbowed back.

"Daniel . . . Suzannah—" Uncle Franklin's tone said unmistakably, *No roughhousing in the stagecoach.*

She nodded. So did Daniel.

Just then the stage driver stepped up to the door. Turning his head, he spat a thin stream of tobacco juice, then doffed his hat and made a mock bow to the passengers. "The name is Otis Mout," he said. "I'm here to say that we got a long ways to go, and I got a schedule to keep. I got only one rule: Don't keep me waitin'."

With that he pulled on yellow gauntlets up to his elbows and announced, "Let's hit the road!" A moment later, he could be heard shouting to the horses from the driver's box. "Git along, boys! Git along!"

The stagecoach lurched forward, setting off through the outskirts of Frederick, and Suzannah's heart raced as she hung on to her seat. All of her life she'd heard of the National Road, and now she was actually riding on it! She pulled aside the window covering and watched the countryside fly by. They were on their way to Independence, Missouri—to the frontier!

Feeling the chill from the open window, she said to Daniel, "Charles must be getting cold up top."

"Wouldn't be surprised," he replied.

The boy seated next to Daniel looked across at her with a shy smile. "He's not sittin' on the driver's box."

Until now, Suzannah had paid little attention to the boy who appeared to be no more than eight. His straight brown hair hung in his eyes so that she could see them only when he looked up. His feet, shod in heavy boots at least two sizes too large for him, dangled a few inches from the floor.

"How would you know?" she asked, curious.

" 'Cause Otis Mout is my uncle." The boy hung his head as if ashamed of the fact. "It's my cousin Joad who's sittin' up there with him."

"Your cousin Joad?"

His gray eyes met hers as he nodded. "The one who helped load the baggage. I'm Timmy Mout," he added. "They're takin' me to my aunt's in Vandalia, Illinois."

"Where's Charles?" Suzannah called to Pauline across the racket of the jostling stagecoach.

Pauline put a warning finger to her lips that clearly said, *Hush!*

"Don't worry," Daniel muttered. "Charles will take care of himself."

Suzannah made a face. "He always does."

On the other side of Daniel, Timmy Mout said sadly, "My folks just died."

Suzannah stared at him, taken by surprise.

"Of the fevers," Timmy explained. "I was sick too, but I'm all right now."

He did look pale, and Daniel backed away just a trifle. "Sure sorry to hear it, Timmy," he said finally. "But glad that you . . . pulled through."

"Me too," Suzannah said.

She really was glad, but the last thing she wanted to do was to talk about parents dying. If hers were still alive, she'd be snug at home in Alexandria right now . . . or in school with her friends.

Now that she thought of it, what would her friends be saying about her family's sudden disappearance? She could imagine Jenny and the rest of them discussing it on the walk to school. "When's the last time you saw them?" they'd ask each other. And—

Best to put them out of mind, Suzannah decided. Word would be out soon enough about Charles's gambling debts. Then everyone would know that her family had left Alexandria in disgrace.

She escaped again to her window. Pulling the leather curtain aside, she saw that patches of snow still dotted the ground here too, but the cold wind hitting her face made her feel better.

Leaning over her shoulder, Daniel pointed out their westward progress on the numbered iron mileposts. "We'll be getting fresh horses soon," he explained importantly. "Every fifteen or twenty miles all the way down the Road, we'll change teams."

It was amazing to watch as Otis Mout drove their stagecoach to the stage relay station where a new team of six horses stood harnessed and waiting along the roadside. The moment he drew the horses to a full stop, Otis threw down the reins to a stagecoach man who exchanged the teams in a swift maneuver, then threw the reins back to Otis. "Git along, boys!" he yelled and drove away with not a second wasted.

West of Hagerstown, they stopped for fresh horses again. As the horses were exchanged, the folks nearby stopped to watch the excitement.

"Look!" Timmy said. "They're all waving at us."

"Let's wave back then," Suzannah said. Even little Jamie joined in, waving his chubby hand.

As the morning passed, Suzannah took a turn holding Jamie while Pauline napped. It wasn't easy. Awake, he squirmed like a puppy trying to get down, and, sleeping, he grew so heavy that her arms ached.

By midday, Suzannah's empty stomach growled in protest. Jolting along all morning hadn't helped a bit either. She felt as seasick as if she had been on a boat.

Noticing her discomfort, Uncle Franklin came to the rescue. "Let me hold that little rascal for a while."

Suzannah handed Jamie over gladly.

Putting up the hood on her cloak, she pulled aside the leather curtain once more and felt the welcome blast of fresh air in her face. As she looked back, she noticed a familiar figure on horseback, riding just far enough behind to avoid the clouds of dust kicked up by churning hooves and rolling wheels.

Charles!

She leaned her head out a bit farther to make sure.

Yes, it was her brother-in-law riding his favorite chestnut. He hadn't given up Lucky after all. Besides, he would sooner give up his family than his horse! No one seemed to be following him anyway. Suzannah let the curtain drop and breathed a sigh of relief.

———◆—◆—◆———

At one o'clock the stage pulled into a curving gravel entry road leading to a wayside inn. Charles had passed them three mileposts back, so by the time they arrived,

Lucky was already tied to the hitching post near two bright green stagecoaches.

Uncle Franklin stood by the door to assist the passengers as they stepped down from the coach. One elderly man stopped to shake Uncle Franklin's hand. "Thank you kindly, sir," he said. "I don't envy you none, ridin' over them mountains this time of year. 'Tis a dangerous journey."

"I expect we'll survive," Uncle Franklin said.

The man cast a worried look at the sky to the west. "Looks to me like blizzards lurkin' in them mountains. Still not too late in the season fer some good ones."

Blizzards! A pang of fear shot through Suzannah. She hadn't even thought of that danger.

Inside the inn, Joad grabbed Timmy roughly by the arm. "We eat in the barroom, not with passengers."

Timmy turned a pleading look in Suzannah's direction, but Joad tugged him toward the barroom door.

"Why don't you pick on someone your own size?" Daniel asked.

Joad shot him a poisonous glance and moved on.

Poor Timmy. The fact that he was an orphan like her touched her deeply. Suzannah wished she could help him somehow.

At that moment, however, the jovial innkeeper appeared to escort them into the dining room. "Any other time of year, these rooms are packed with travelers," he said, taking them to a round table. "Lines of them waitin' to come in. Usually seven stagecoaches to the mile along the Road, and Conestoga freight wagons, farm wagons, and buggies."

"I hear that drovers herd hundreds of cattle and hogs and sheep right down the Road," Aunt Ruthie remarked.

"Yes, indeed," the innkeeper replied as he seated her. "Even turkeys."

"They drive *turkeys* along the Road?" Suzannah asked.

"Yes, miss. There's special inns for drovers, with pens and fields for their beasts. Keeps 'em from fightin' with the wagoners."

"The wagoners fight the drovers?" Daniel asked.

The innkeeper nodded. "Wagoners don't take kindly to cattle, sheep, or hogs slowin' 'em down. Turkeys are worse yet, flutterin' all over the Road."

"That's nothing," Daniel said to Suzannah. "I heard there were herds of buffalo here years ago."

"Oh, come on, Daniel. You're joking."

"Not one bit," the innkeeper put in. "That's how the Road started. Buffalo came for fresh pastures and salt licks, and the Injuns followed. Finally, the white man saw it was the best trail over the Allegheny Mountains."

Charles, coming from the nearby barroom, overheard the innkeeper. "Sounds reasonable," he said. Seating himself, he turned to Suzannah. "I'm sure *you* must know all about the Road from your girls' school."

Was he *trying* to aggravate her, using that tone of voice? she wondered. She forced herself to speak calmly. "Only that Thomas Jefferson worried about losing the wilderness to France. He thought a national east-west road would bind the states into one big country."

"Jefferson was right," Uncle Franklin agreed.

"Any man with grit and muscle can have good farmin' land for next to nothin' just off the Road," the innkeeper added.

Suzannah glanced at Charles. He had plenty of grit for gambling. But the last thing he'd want to do was use his muscles for hard farm labor.

Everyone was still discussing the virtues of the Road when the innkeeper's wife brought out their roast beef, potatoes with gravy, and biscuits. Once they were served, Uncle Franklin asked Charles to say grace.

"I defer to you," Charles replied smoothly.

Uncle Franklin nodded, and they bowed their heads. "Almighty God, Our Heavenly Father," he began in his nice deep voice. "We come before Thee with praise and thanksgiving for a safe trip thus far—"

Feeling Charles's eyes on her, Suzannah peeked through her lashes at him. His hands were folded reverently enough, but his eyes were wide open. When they met her gaze, he gave her a wink as if to say, *We don't believe in that nonsense, do we?*

She blinked her eyes shut. Why should she be surprised? He had never attended Christ Church in Alexandria with the family. And, at home, he had always encouraged them to pray privately before meals. It was perfectly clear to Suzannah. Charles Herrington just pretended to be a believer, but he was not one at all!

After their hearty "Amen," Jamie banged the table. "Eat!" he called out.

Everyone laughed. But Suzannah, looking up, caught the eye of the mean-looking boy staring at her from the bar-room. *Joad!* He'd seen them praying, and now sent her a scornful look.

Daniel noticed, too. "I hope we're not going to have trouble with him."

"Exactly what I was thinking," Suzannah said. First there was the threat of blizzards, and now she had Joad to deal with. This trip might turn out to be even more difficult than she'd imagined.

CHAPTER

Talk at the dinner table was lively, so no one even noticed when Suzannah grew unusually quiet. Lest Charles give her another dirty look, she took pains not to glance in his direction throughout the entire meal, but kept her eyes on her own plate.

"None for me, thank you," Aunt Ruthie told the serving girl when she brought thick slabs of steaming apple pie topped with cream for dessert. "As you can see, I've had a few too many sweets already."

There was good-natured laughter all around.

"And, Suzannah dear," Aunt Ruthie continued, noting the generous serving of pie her niece had accepted, "do remember that you'll be bouncing in a stagecoach all afternoon!"

"Oh, I'll be fine. Father said I had an ironclad stomach. Maybe Daniel and I could split your slice—"

Aunt Ruthie handed her piece of pie over. "You're a fast talker when you want to be, Suzannah Colton."

Uncle Franklin had a mischievous glint in his green eyes as he hummed a bar or two of "Oh, Suzannah!" But to her relief, Timmy came in from the barroom just before her uncle broke into the familiar chorus.

"Uncle Otis says we'll be leaving in five or ten minutes."

"Would you like half my pie, Timmy? It's too much for me," Pauline offered, noticing his thin frame as he sidled up to the table.

Timmy's eyes widened. "Yes'm, if you're sure you can't eat it—"

Suzannah made room for Timmy on the bench next to her. While everyone was finishing dessert, she gave him some advice. "Aunt Ruthie and Uncle Franklin will help you in any way they can. They believe in 'doing unto others as you'd have them do unto you.' "

Timmy smiled a little as he forked his pie in, but Uncle Franklin gave her a peculiar look.

When they were ready to board the stagecoach again, Timmy hurried along beside Uncle Franklin. "What can you tell by lookin' at a person?" he asked. "Like, if a person's a thief or a liar, can you tell by just lookin' at him?"

Uncle Franklin lifted his eyebrows. "If a man's truly wicked, he often can't keep the badness from his face any more than a good man can hide his goodness," he replied. "Still, you can't always count on it. Evil wears disguises sometimes. It can look mighty good, can even be beautiful or handsome."

Like Charles, Suzannah thought.

"Why do you ask, son?"

Timmy shrugged, but his eyes were full of worry. "Just wonderin' about my relations in Vandalia."

"We'll take care of you, Timmy," Suzannah said.

When Timmy had climbed into the stagecoach, Uncle Franklin pulled Suzannah to one side. "I'd like a word with you."

Puzzled, she followed him toward the back of the stage-coach.

"I know you mean to reassure Timmy," Uncle Franklin told her, "and it's true that we can help him now. But we can't control what happens to him in Vandalia—only God can do that."

Suzannah nodded. Still, she intended to look out for Timmy while she could.

By the time they climbed aboard the coach, a new passenger was sitting on the middle seat. "Mrs. Fortran," she introduced herself as the others took their seats. "I'm on my way to Vandalia, Illinois."

"You're going there, too?" Timmy asked, wide-eyed.

"Indeed I am," she replied. "Going to stay with my son and his wife and grandsons. I'd guess one of them's about your age."

"Eight?" Timmy asked, hopeful.

"Exactly," she replied. "A good boy, too. Not a ruffian like the big one who loaded my luggage. Why, he eyed my gold brooch like he could already feel it in his pocket."

"Joad," Suzannah said. "He's Timmy's cousin."

Since her shoulder had begun to ache from the weight of the traveling bag, she had put it down between her feet for a rest. Thinking of Joad Mout, she pressed her feet together to feel the traveling bag.

They were just about to set off when a buggy wheeled up with another passenger. "Beggin' your pardon for the delay," said the elderly man, climbing in. "Just barely made it." He sat down next to Mrs. Fortran. "The name's Gabe Multon," he added, panting, "and I come from the state o' Delaware."

He tipped his hat and nodded politely as the door was shut. Mr. Multon was short and wiry, and his merry face and rumpled brown suit reminded Suzannah of an elf.

Uncle Franklin introduced everyone, to which Gabe Multon replied, "A pleasure to meet you, I'm sure."

Outside, Otis Mout cracked the whip over the horses. "Git along! Git along, boys!"

The stagecoach jerked forward once more, and they all clung to their seats. "Onward to them mountains!" Gabe shouted over the racket. "Let's hope there's no blizzards!"

"Don't even mention such a thing!" said Mrs. Fortran with a shudder of her solid frame.

"Do you know these parts, Mr. Multon?" called out Uncle Franklin from the back seat.

"That I do. Drove a peddlin' wagon on the National Road between Baltimore and Vandalia for many a year. Thought I'd try it once by stagecoach to see my kinfolk in Illinois."

Aunt Ruthie, who had been a teacher, beamed. "Oh, then perhaps you would be so kind as to tell us what you know about the Road as we go along?"

Gabe gave a nod, then pulled aside a curtain to peer out the window. "Johnny Appleseed himself roamed these parts. Fact is, those apple trees alongside the Road are thought to be some he planted. Come spring, they'll be a pretty sight to see!"

Since Suzannah had heard all about Johnny Appleseed in school, she leaned back and closed her eyes for a nap, lulled by the rocking motion of the carriage and the effects of the big meal she had just eaten. But Gabe's next outburst jolted her awake.

"Skin your eyes now! There's a wagonhouse for freight drivers! I stayed many a night at places like that when I was a-peddlin'. Cheaper . . . and hearty food. But they don't warm much to stagecoachers."

"Why not?" Daniel asked.

"'Spect they think stagecoachers is uppity." The old man chuckled. "And now it 'pears I'm one of you."

As they drove on into the foothills of the mountains, the temperature dropped abruptly. The passengers snapped their leather curtains shut, and everyone pulled the buffalo robes up to their chins. For once, Suzannah was glad for the double layer of petticoats and the kid boots that buttoned halfway up her legs.

Looking out the window, she saw horses covered with great capes of goatskin or scraped bear hide to protect them from the cold. And, at the next relay station, their fresh team was bundled in scraped bear hides, too.

As night fell, they stopped at another wayside inn. Weary from the day's travel, Pauline asked that food be sent up to the room for herself and Jamie.

"Do you mind company?" Suzannah asked and got a nod from Pauline and Aunt Ruthie. Besides the ache in every bone of her body, Suzannah would just as soon avoid another run-in with Charles. As it was, she was grateful that he had chosen to ride Lucky alongside the stagecoach most of the time.

Soon, one day blended into the next. Mornings, they ate a hearty breakfast, then traveled along the Road, changing horses every two hours or so until the midday dinner stop. After that, it was another long ride until nightfall.

One day, out of pure boredom, Timmy made a suggestion. "Let's show what we've got in our pockets. I'll go first." He brought out a bag of marbles, a small red ball, a wallet, and a dirty, creased letter from his aunt in Vandalia.

Daniel produced a wallet, a red bandanna handkerchief, and coins from one pocket. From the other, his true colors surfaced when he pulled out a jackknife for whittling, a sturdy slingshot, fishhooks, and a ball of fishing string.

"Now it's your turn, Suzannah," said Timmy.

She kept her traveling bag under her cloak. But in the pockets, she found a white handkerchief, spare blue mittens to match her cloak, and some old ribbons for her braids. "Not much," she admitted. "Only interesting thing about it is that Pauline made the mittens."

"What about your traveling bag?"

"You said *pockets*," Suzannah told Timmy firmly. "A lady's traveling bag is private."

"Lady?" Daniel laughed, so she had to give him a poke in the ribs.

She was glad when the subject changed to fishing. Worrying about her gold coins made her feel like an old miser, but they also gave her courage.

———◆◆◆———

From the Allegheny foothills, they wound their way into the mountains. Along the Road snow lay thickly on the boughs of great pines. "That snow is here to stay," Gabe said. "Those tall trees hide it from the sun."

At midday, as Suzannah stepped out of the farmhouse inn, she looked up into heavy, bleak clouds. Drifting lazily from the clouds were large, white flakes. "It's snowing!" she exclaimed. "Isn't it beautiful?"

"Can't say as I like the looks of it," Otis Mout said. "We better git movin'."

Snow fell more heavily as they rode higher into the mountains, quieting the rattle of the stagecoach. They peered out only occasionally at the snowstorm. After a while the stagecoach slowed considerably. "It's apt to turn into a full blizzard in the Cumberland Gap," said Gabe.

"It doesn't look good," Uncle Franklin agreed, "but we have a fine driver."

"Maybe we'll never get through the mountains!" said Mrs. Fortran, her voice rising in alarm.

"Hush," Gabe warned her. "You'll scare the children."

Before long, the coach slowed even more and then came to a stop. Gabe pulled aside a snow-encrusted window curtain. Outside Charles was making for the back of the stagecoach. "Looks like he'll tie his horse to the coach and ride inside fer a spell."

"Thank goodness," Pauline said through her muffler.

A blast of cold and snow blew in when Charles entered the coach. "The weather's worsening," he announced. He pulled the door shut against the wind and sat down between Mrs. Fortran and Gabe Multon, facing Suzannah. Snow clung to his gray hat and wool coat, and his nose was red with cold. He brushed off the snow and pulled a buffalo robe up over his shoulders.

Suzannah was relieved when he closed his eyes. When Charles was awake, there was always the chance of an argument.

The snowstorm was roaring through the Gap now, buffeting the stagecoach. Gusts of wind and snow whipped at the window curtains, and the coach took the winding turns with more caution. At long last they stopped completely.

Otis Mout opened the coach door, raising his voice above the wind. "We'll put up at this Cumberland Gap wagonhouse! We got high drifts, so we're parked nearer the stables than the wagonhouse."

"But I thought wagonhouses were only for freighters—" Suzannah began.

"They won't turn us out in this weather," Gabe assured her.

Charles was the first one out. "I have to tend to Lucky," he said as he swept past Pauline and Jamie.

What about his family? Suzannah thought, clenching her fists.

A second thought occurred to her. If those men came after him again, he could make a faster getaway on a horse than in a stagecoach. No wonder Lucky was so important!

"I'll help Mrs. Fortran down," Gabe said to Uncle Franklin, "so you can tend to your own family."

"Good thinking," Uncle Franklin replied, then turned to them. "Mufflers up over your faces and caps down over your ears. We'll have to hold onto each other." He climbed out into the blinding snow and opened his arms for Jamie, who was so bundled up that only his big blue eyes and nose peeped out.

Aunt Ruthie climbed down and held onto Uncle Franklin's other arm. Next came Pauline, then Suzannah and Daniel, all clinging together, heads lowered against the driving snow and wind. Last came Gabe, helping Mrs. Fortran.

The horses whinnied as Otis Mout and Joad led them away toward the stables. At least Suzannah assumed that's where they were going.

As Uncle Franklin led them through the whirling whiteness toward the inn, Suzannah glanced back. Timmy stood at the stagecoach door alone, probably expecting his uncle and cousin to come for him. At the last moment she heard his pitiful plea, "Wait for me!"

"Hurry!" Suzannah called to him through the icy blasts of snow.

In his rush, Timmy fell headlong into a snowdrift, and Suzannah reached out to help him up.

"Come on!" Daniel said, grabbing one of Timmy's mittened hands, while Suzannah took the other.

Hearing voices, the three hurried to catch up, stumbling through drifts, slipping on icy ruts. Suddenly Suzannah lost her footing and fell. Her head cracked against something, and silvery stars spun in her head.

At last—how long she could not be sure—she came to herself and sat up, icy snow needles pelting her cold face. There was no one in sight. No one at all. Not a sound could be heard above the constant roar of wind through the pines.

Suzannah was absolutely alone. Not even her ever-present travel bag gave her much comfort. What use was money—even gold—when you were lost in a snowstorm?

She looked about her, trying to get her bearings. Even if there had been familiar landmarks, they would have been erased by the snow. The entire landscape—earth and sky—was a blinding white.

"Help!" Suzannah cried, her voice muffled by the roaring blizzard. "Help!"

There was no answer. Only the wind, driving the snow ahead of it, blustered.

She stood up shakily, calling out again, cupping her mouth with a mittened hand. Still no answer.

She must find the coach. Surely it was close by. She wandered blindly in one direction, then another. No coach or horses. Tears sprang to her eyes, and she brushed them away with snow-caked mittens.

Perhaps if she walked in a circle, an ever-expanding circle, she would find the coach or even the wagonhouse. Surely someone would come for her.

"Help!" she called out again into the storm.

She started to her right, beginning the circle, although in this all-white world it was impossible to know where she had been or where she was going. Almost as soon as she took a step through the heavy drift, her footprint would be covered over by the rapidly falling snow. She had heard of animals being caught in just this kind of sudden storm, their bodies not to be seen again until spring! Wouldn't Jenny be surprised to hear that she had never made it to the frontier, that she'd been buried by a blizzard in the mountains?

No! She mustn't think like that. She just couldn't! What would become of Pauline and little Jamie if anything happened to her?

She stomped her cold feet to keep the circulation going. Then ducking her head into the wind, she forced her way onward. At long last, one outstretched hand touched something solid. A rope—a snow rope?

Suzannah had heard of pioneers who'd use ropes to guide them to their livestock during snowstorms. The rope was usually fastened to the cabin door and led to the barn. She just hoped she had stumbled onto one of them . . . not onto some kind of animal trap.

Pulling herself forward, hand over hand, Suzannah finally made out the blurred silhouette of an outbuilding. Hurrying as fast as she could through the snow, she felt her way along the rope until she turned a corner and was sheltered from the snowy blasts.

A stable! Otis Mout had mentioned stables. This must be one of them. She heard a horse whinnying inside and saw a door ahead.

Tugging at the latch, she opened it just wide enough to let herself in, then pushed the door shut against the storm. Leaning weakly against it, she caught her breath. The smell of damp hay and horses filled her cold nose, choking her. At least she wouldn't freeze to death in here. She already felt warmer.

"Suzannah—"

Was that Daniel's voice? Or was she imagining it?

She felt the lump on the side of her head. Ouch! That was real enough. Horses whinnied and stirred.

After a moment the stable door opened, and Daniel and Timmy tumbled in. They were covered with snow, but glad to see her.

Daniel pulled down his muffler. "We heard you yell and tried to answer, but the wind must have carried the sound of our voices the other way."

Suzannah shook her head, still a bit dizzy. "I fell and hit my head. When I came to, I couldn't see anyone."

"You all right?" Daniel asked.

"I am now. But how will we find the others? And the wagonhouse?"

"They disappeared in the storm after I turned back for you and Timmy," Daniel said.

Timmy hung his head. "It's my fault. I thought Uncle Otis or Joad would come for me, but when they didn't—"

"It's not your fault," Suzannah said. "It's not your fault at all. Your uncle should have told you—"

"The question now is what we should do," Daniel interrupted.

Through her dizziness, Suzannah remembered. "I found a rope that led me here to the stable. It may connect to the wagonhouse."

"A snow rope!" Timmy said. "At the last inn Uncle Otis talked with other drivers about using snow ropes to find their way in snowstorms."

They opened the stable door, and a cold blast of whirling snow hit them. "There it is!" Suzannah exclaimed. "That's the one!"

"Let's go!" Daniel took charge, but for a change, he didn't sound impatient or bossy. "Stay close to each other, but hang on to that rope! Ready?"

"Ready!" said Suzannah and Timmy in one breath, then pulled up their mufflers.

"Follow me."

They stepped out into the snowstorm, the wind almost taking their breath away. With Daniel and Timmy struggling on ahead of Suzannah, it wasn't nearly as difficult as when she'd been lost in the whiteness alone.

Daniel, looking like a snowman, glanced back from time to time, then forged ahead. Suzannah and Timmy followed close in his footsteps, holding onto the snow rope.

"Listen!" Daniel halted, holding up a hand. "Do you hear anything?"

Timmy and Suzannah paused, listening. The storm had not let up for a minute. But through the roar could be heard a faint ringing noise.

"Sounds like a school bell!" she called out.

Pressing on, they continued in the direction of the sound until they saw a log house, as beautiful to them as if it had been a mansion built of marble. A brass bell hung high over the front door was ringing furiously. Below it, a red-faced man pulled the bell rope with all his might.

"You the Colton young'uns?" he called when he caught sight of them.

"Yes!" they called back through chattering teeth.

"And Timmy Mout!"

"Thank the good Lord you're safe!" cried the man. "Now git on in here and thaw out!"

Safe inside the log wagonhouse, they looked around for the sight of familiar faces. Aunt Ruthie rushed forward and caught all three of them in her arms. "Praise God, you're safe! Uncle Franklin and Charles have gone out looking for you with Otis and Joad Mout."

"They couldn't have gotten far," the innkeeper said. "I stopped ringin' the bell so's to let the men know the young'uns had been found. 'Spect they'll be along directly."

"Come on, children," Aunt Ruthie said. "Come over by the fire and get warm."

For once, Suzannah didn't mind Aunt Ruthie's mothering one bit. Shedding soggy wraps, the three of them hurried to the huge stone fireplace and put out their hands to its blazing warmth. Giant sparks popped and crackled as the flames licked at the logs.

As they stood warming themselves, a serving girl rushed over with mugs of steaming cider. Never had hot apple cider tasted so good, Suzannah decided.

Moments later Uncle Franklin came in the door. "Thanks be to God, you're safe!" he exclaimed when he saw them. He hugged Suzannah, then Daniel and Timmy.

Coming in the door behind him, even Charles looked grateful. But before he could say anything, Otis and Joad Mout rushed in, stamping their snowy boots by the door.

"There he is!" Otis muttered, pointing at Timmy and clouting Joad on the arm. "I told you to keep an eye out fer the boy!"

Joad winced, grabbing his arm, then glared at Timmy. *Oh, oh,* Suzannah thought.

Before long, travelers from other stagecoaches stopped by the storm joined them to tell of their trials in the blizzard. Everyone had a story to tell—from the weathered wagon driver with a lame horse to a well-dressed passenger from the South who had never before seen a snowflake!

Suzannah glanced around the group, feeling a special kinship with each one. There was a friendly atmosphere of caring and concern. Captured for this time by the storm outside, these strangers had become family.

Suzannah's head began to nod. Then Daniel poked her. "Look at Joad," he whispered.

The tall boy glowered at them from the shadows at the back of the room.

"Looks like he's plotting some evil scheme to get even with us," Suzannah whispered to Daniel.

CHAPTER 4

"That it does," her cousin agreed.

"Wish I knew why he hates us so much," she said, half to Daniel and half to herself. A shiver passed over her, but this time it wasn't caused by the blizzard.

CHAPTER 5

The blizzard was still raging outside when they sat down at a long plank table to an enormous supper. There were platters heaped with roasted beef and venison, bowls mounded with mashed potatoes, baskets brimming with hot biscuits and muffins—not to mention gravy, pickles, jams, and jelly.

By the time the dried-peach cobbler was served, Suzannah had forgotten Joad entirely. "I'm glad this wagon-house welcomed even 'uppity' stagecoach passengers today!"

"Amen," Uncle Franklin agreed. "They'll be singing around the fireplace after supper, too." His green eyes lit up with mischief. "No doubt we'll have a rousing chorus or two of your favorite song, Suzannah."

"Ugh!" She knew he liked to tease her with her name-song. "I've already heard it a thousand times!"

"Well, I expect you'll hear it again," her uncle said.

After supper, a wagoner brought out his fiddle, and Uncle Franklin took out his harmonica. Once again, everyone settled around the roaring fire, and someone started singing:

We heard of Ohio,
We heard of the Road,
We crossed the stern mountains,
With the lightest of load—

When the song died down, the fiddler struck up another chord.

Oh, hustle along, my six-horse team,
Up the mountain and over the stream!
Pull the big wagon, best you know—
Pull till we cross the O-h-i-o—

After a few more songs, Uncle Franklin launched into a familiar melody. Suzannah cringed, then joined in herself, bobbing her head comically as she sang:

Oh, I come from Alabama with my banjo on my knee,
And I'm going to Louisiana, my true love for to see.
It rained all night the day I left;
The weather it was dry.
The sun so hot I froze to death;
Suzannah don't you cry.
Oh Suzannah, don't you cry for me;
I've come from Alabama with my banjo on my knee.

On the chorus, all eyes turned toward Suzannah. As if that weren't bad enough, one of the wagoners danced out on the wooden floor and clogged in time to the music, bowing low to her.

When the song ended, Suzannah clapped with the others. It could be vexing to have your name in a song, but sometimes it was fun too. She could see that Uncle Franklin was proud that she took the teasing so well. The only one who sat back in the corner and didn't join in, she noticed, was Joad Mout. Even Charles and Otis Mout sang heartily.

"Best rendition of 'Oh, Suzannah!' I've ever heard!" Daniel said. "Let's sing it again!"

"Daniel's heading for the lion's den," warned Suzannah, using one of Uncle Franklin's pet phrases.

Her cousin grinned broadly. "Never mind then!"

"Uh-oh! Look who's going to sing now," Suzannah said, nodding toward the fireplace. Charles, who fancied himself an opera singer, was standing in front of the roaring fire, waiting for the hilarity to die down.

"Oh, no, not that!" Daniel moaned.

"Wouldn't you know! He's showing off again." Suzannah could barely control her disgust.

When the audience had settled down again, Charles announced, "I shall render the light and happy aria from *Rigoletto*—'La donna è mobile,' which means 'Woman is fickle.' "

"Hmmph!" Suzannah said to Daniel. "Charles isn't so dependable himself."

As he began to sing, the wagoners and others began to leave, saying "Think I'll turn in" and "We'd better rest up if we expect to dig out in the morning!"

Even Uncle Franklin and Aunt Ruthie, who were usually so patient, rose the moment Charles finished.

"Time for bed," Uncle Franklin announced with an "Enough is enough!" tone in his voice.

Charles's singing, as might be expected, ended the evening's festivities.

The blizzard stopped during the night, too. When the travelers went out the next morning, they were relieved to see that the wind had blown much of the snow into the forests on either side of the road.

Otis Mout scanned the clear skies. "Looks like we might be able to move on. We'll let the Conestoga freight wagons lead the way. They've got stronger teams, even if they are slower."

For breakfast they ate from plates piled high with eggs, ham, bacon, and flapjacks. "Eat hearty," the wagonhouse keeper told them. "Don't know when you'll be eatin' again."

"At least we'll die with a full stomach," Mrs. Fortran said as they climbed into their stagecoach and started out again through the snow-covered countryside.

"Hush!" Gabe warned her again. "The young'uns!"

Suzannah and Daniel exchanged annoyed glances. She, for one, wasn't that fearful, but Timmy was, and she didn't want anything else to worry him.

The Conestoga wagons had already cut tracks through the drifts in the wagonhouse yard and on the Road. In places, though, the Road was icy, and their stagecoach would slide precariously toward the edge. Then, while the passengers held their breath and leaned toward the opposite side, the stage would slide back toward the middle of the Road.

Once past the Gap, they followed the trail General Braddock made on his way to fight the French. Gabe Multon pointed out Braddock's gravesite and Fort Necessity, where the French beat George Washington.

Day after day they drove on westward, making less than their usual ten miles an hour. At Grantsville, they crossed over the famous Casselman Bridge, the largest single-span stone arch in the whole country. Then they turned north toward Pennsylvania.

Dense forests covered the snowy slopes of the Allegheny Mountains until suddenly the Road broke from the trees. Stretching out before them was an awesome sight—low hills threaded with rivers and towns and church steeples shimmering in the sunshine.

"Guess I'll get out at the next stop and ride awhile. Warm enough now to be out," Charles said, stretching his tall frame and making for the door of the coach.

But before he could make a quick exit, Uncle Franklin caught hold of his coat sleeve. "See to it that you don't look for . . . the wrong companions."

Charles shook him off. "That's my affair."

"You gave me your word." Uncle Franklin's gaze was firm and direct.

Charles shot him a dark look, but said nothing more. When he left, Suzannah felt relieved. It made her nervous to see Charles always glancing back over his shoulder as if those men were still behind him. Later, when she looked back, she saw that he kept pace with the stagecoach, dutifully stopping at Uniontown and Washington with them.

As they rode on, Mrs. Fortran complained, "I do wish Mr. Mout wouldn't drive so fast."

Gabe Multon laughed. "That's why they call these coaches 'shake guts'!"

Mrs. Fortran looked at him askance. "Tsk, tsk, such language, Mr. Multon! And before ladies and children, too!"

Gabe put a gloved hand to his mouth. "Fergot myself. Beggin' your pardon, ma'am."

Suzannah hid a smile behind her mittened hand.

Gabe's word for coaches was exactly right. Her "insides" were sure shaken up from all the bouncing.

They drove on in a flurry of snow to Wheeling, where the Ohio River twined through the valley like a silver ribbon. "I'm eager to do some exploring," Daniel said to Suzannah. "Looks like we might have time when we get there."

"Count me in," Suzannah said.

When they drove up at the Wheeling Hotel, she asked, "You want to come along, Timmy?"

"Sure," he said, "if Uncle Otis will let me."

After the baggage was settled in their rooms and promises had been made to be back before dark, the three of them met outside the hotel. The snow flurries had stopped, and the town glowed pink and gold in the late afternoon sun.

"I thought Wheeling was only a river town," Suzannah said as they strolled down the main street, "but just look at this . . . pottery works and a broom factory!"

Farther on there was a woolen mill, and tanneries that reeked of drying hides. As they passed the fish market, Daniel said, "Tonight I'm going to ask for catfish. Gabe says Ohio catfish are so big that they have to cut 'em in half before they'll fit into the biggest skillets."

"Oh, Daniel!" Suzannah protested. "If we saw a catfish that big, I'd really have to *skin my eyes,* as Gabe says." They all laughed.

Walking on a bit, Timmy spoke up. "Uncle Otis says Wheeling is called 'Nail City.'"

"Truly?" Suzannah asked.

He nodded, serious as ever. "He said coopers work day and night just to make enough kegs for the nails they ship out."

"Hey, let's look for a nail factory," Daniel said, walking on ahead.

"How has Joad been treating you since we got lost in the blizzard?" Suzannah asked Timmy.

The boy shrugged his thin shoulders. "He doesn't like me. Says he's going to get me yet."

"But why doesn't he like you?"

Timmy shook his head. "Because I don't have to work for my passage like him. Some other reasons too. My father was a teacher, and Joad says I put on airs."

"Why, you don't put on airs at all!" Suzannah said. "In fact, I thought you were shy until I got to know you."

"I guess I am, a little," Timmy said. "At least that's what my mother always claimed." His expression grew sad. "But most of all, I miss my folks."

Suzannah nodded. "I know. Mine are dead too. After a while, though, you get more used to it. You'll just have to learn to take care of yourself, like I had to do. Pauline gives in to everything."

"I'm not so good at being tough, either."

"Well, it takes practice," Suzannah said. "I'm getting better and better at it . . . maybe because I have to be tough for Pauline and Jamie."

Catching up to Daniel, they saw the nail factories Timmy's uncle had told him about. Burly workmen rolled hundreds of kegs of nails onto the Conestoga freight wagons lined up out front. Ahead, smoke rose from iron foundries, their furnaces stoked with Wheeling coal.

Suddenly Timmy turned and, looking behind him, pointed. "There's Joad!"

Sure enough, Joad Mout was following them on the opposite side of the street.

"I still wonder why he's so mean," Suzannah said.

Timmy shrugged. "Uncle Otis says you got to make allowances for him 'cause his ma just up and left them."

Suzannah drew a deep breath. "At least my parents didn't leave us on purpose," she said. Feeling a pang of sympathy for Joad, she called back to him, "You want to come with us?"

People on the sidewalk turned to look, but Joad pretended not to hear.

"Hey, Joad!" she shouted again and repeated the invitation.

He kept his eyes straight ahead.

"He can't say we didn't try to be friendly," she told Daniel. "I just thought it might help Timmy."

"So much for your always wanting to control everything," he said.

"At least I tried." Suzannah thought about what Daniel had said. Was it true that she really wanted to control everything? That would take some thought.

"If Joad's going to be like that," Daniel said, taking charge himself, "as soon as that wagon rolls between us, let's duck down by the river and hide from him!" He waited until just the right moment, then gave the order. "All right . . . now!"

They rushed down the embankment and hid behind a copse of pine trees. When they peered through the trees, they saw Joad up above, looking all around for them.

Suzannah whispered, "He's just going to be madder than ever."

"I knew he wouldn't come with us," Timmy said. "Uncle Otis is a little rough maybe, but Joad doesn't like folks. He's just plain mean."

After a while Joad gave up the search and left, and the three of them stood by the river. The sun had begun to settle against the forested skyline, splashing the river with bright golds, oranges, and reds.

"I wish Pauline were here to see this," Suzannah said wistfully. "She'd sketch it, and then we'd have it to remember this afternoon forever."

Daniel turned to look into her face. "You really love your sister, don't you?"

Suzannah nodded. "Of course I do. But sometimes I get so mad at her for giving in to Charles that I could scream."

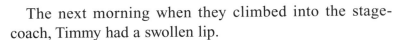

The next morning when they climbed into the stagecoach, Timmy had a swollen lip.

"Did Joad hit you?" Suzannah asked, furious at the big bully.

Timmy stared at his boots. "Don't want to talk about it."

When Uncle Franklin caught her eye, Suzannah decided it was best not to meddle at the moment. She looked out the window as the stagecoach lurched onward toward the rushing river.

Nearing the riverbank, Suzannah saw a ferry creeping toward them across the sunstruck water, reminding her of yesterday's fine outing with Daniel and Timmy.

"Whoa!" Otis Mout yelled. "Whoa, boys!"

The coach drew to a halt, and they all poked their heads out the windows. Behind them, two Conestoga wagons loaded with kegs of nails pulled up.

"Enough nails there to build a few more new towns in the Ohio wilderness," said Gabe.

Their new passenger, Mrs. Gepp, was curious about her destination. "Be it wilderness by Columbus?"

"Not in town," Gabe said. "Columbus is the state capital of O-hi-o, y'know."

"I'm going there to live with family, but I be sceered of bears and sech," the woman said.

"Can't say I blame you," Gabe said. "I've come across more bears than I ever hoped to see right here along the Road. I 'spect they're still in hibernation this time of year though." He chuckled. "Don't worry, Mrs. Gepp. If we see one, I'll wrestle 'im for you."

"I look forward to seeing that!" Uncle Franklin said with a laugh.

Everyone chuckled, but Suzannah felt a little uneasy herself. Bears no longer wandered into Alexandria, but old-timers still told hair-raising stories about them.

She heard the wash of water before she saw what was causing it. "Here it is now—the ferry!"

The wooden, bargelike boat grated gently against the riverbank. "Won't the horses bolt when we board?" she asked Gabe.

"They're used to it. They'll be calmer'n you are."

She had to smile. But she still steeled herself as Otis Mout drove the stagecoach onto the ferry. Before long the river was lapping against the sides of the ferry as it angled to the opposite shore—the Ohio Wilderness.

Being ferried wasn't so bad after all, Suzannah decided, once she had adjusted to the rhythm of the river. In fact Pauline was making use of the time to sketch the sights. When they approached land, Gabe said, "Now you'll see how the Road has opened up the wilderness fer this country o' ours."

After a change of horses, they bounced along through forested countryside bound for Zanesville and then Columbus. For hours at a time, the trail was shaded by thick trees. Once in a while, though, clearings appeared, studded with log houses, barns, and acres of farmland.

Reaching Columbus at last, situated on a sloping rise above the Scioto River, they drove in on Friend Street and stopped at a hotel not far from a new courthouse.

"Now you'll have Sunday to yerselves," Otis Mout said as the passengers left the stage. "See you Monday mornin' . . . early." He turned a stern face to his nephew.

"And, Tim, you ride on with us. We won't be stayin' here."

Timmy climbed back into the coach reluctantly,

"Mr. Mout," Aunt Ruthie interrupted, "I'd like to ask that Timmy attend church with us tomorrow morning. We'd take care of his midday meal as well."

Otis's squinty eyes opened a trifle. "Ain't fittin'—"

"But my folks always took me to church when they—" Timmy choked out.

"I'd take the responsibility for him, Mr. Mout, have no fear," Uncle Franklin put in kindly.

Otis drew a deep breath. "Guess he may as well go with you then. Give me some time off from playin' nursemaid for him."

———◆———

The air was crisp, but the warming sun promised a fine day as the travelers set out for church the next morning. Strolling along the wide brick sidewalk, Uncle Franklin and Aunt Ruthie led the way. Next came Pauline and Jamie with no Charles in sight. Last came Suzannah, Daniel, and Timmy . . . dressed in their best outfits.

"Who'd have thought just a few months ago that we'd be going to church in Columbus, Ohio?" Suzannah asked, enjoying their westering adventure more and more.

"Look at the statehouse!" Pauline said. "Why . . . they've painted the columns to resemble marble."

"The place is flourishing," Uncle Franklin said. "Glad to see our countrymen doing so well in these parts."

In the harbor water lapped at the levees and at the hulls of grimy barges and great white showboats. A flock of pigeons flew toward the city. "Look at the birds!" Aunt Ruthie pointed. "They're a reminder that we're on the edge of the wilderness. In fact, last night a wild turkey tried to get into the hotel!"

"Where *we* stayed, you could hear wolves howling!" Timmy added. "They hunt for food in the back streets."

Suzannah was glad to see that his lip was no longer swollen. "Are your uncle and Joad going to church this morning?"

Timmy shook his head. "They don't much care for it."

"Neither does Charles!" she blurted, then clamped her lips shut at Uncle Franklin's reproving glance.

This very morning she had overheard her uncle and Charles exchange angry words in the hallway of the hotel outside her door. "Can't you control yourself, man?" Uncle Franklin had asked. "Remember your duty to your wife, child, and young sister-in-law!" Unable to hear Charles's mumbled reply, she could only guess that he had been gambling again.

Pushing the bitter scene out of her mind, Suzannah hurried to catch up with Daniel as a peal of bells rang out from the steeple of a white clapboard church. Her dark feelings lifted when she slid into a visitors' pew and heard the organist strike up "Fairest Lord Jesus"—the very hymn Pauline had sung as a solo at their last church service in Alexandria!

Suzannah swallowed hard at the memory, then added her voice to the others: *Ruler of all nature . . .*

She sang on, Pauline's lovely soprano voice on one side of her, Daniel's tenor on the other. Blending in harmony were Uncle Franklin's rich baritone, Aunt Ruthie's alto, and even Timmy's sweet tones. They might be in the wilderness with plenty of problems, but they were all in God's family . . . and all together.

CHAPTER 6

The next morning the sun shone brightly as they pulled out of Columbus with a fresh team of horses. Traffic on the Road was busier than ever, and they were grateful for the cold snap that kept the muddy patches of road frozen solid beneath the horses' hooves. Riders on saddle horses outraced the stagecoach, while drovers driving hundreds of sheep slowed their pace time and again. Caravans of Conestoga freight wagons thundered down the Road, setting off a jingling of bells in the crisp March air.

For the first time, Suzannah noticed an unusual sight. Here and there along the roadside were whole families, some huddled miserably by blazing campfires. The camps smelled of beans, salt pork, and boiled coffee. The men wore tattered britches of linsey-woolsey and patched coats. The women, tight-lipped and stern, went about their chores while the children, seemingly unaware of the cold, romped and played close by.

"The poor dears!" Aunt Ruthie said, a look of sympathy clouding her face.

Gabe said, "They're usually farmers whose land has played out on them back home. They're hopin' to settle their families where the soil is richer for growin' better crops."

Uncle Franklin looked at their overloaded farm wagons. "From the looks of things the trip is likely to take them a long time . . . if they make it at all."

Just at that moment, their attention was diverted by a commotion up ahead.

"Stagecoach turned over! Whoa, boys!" called Otis Mout. He brought the coach to a fast stop near the upturned vehicle.

Suzannah's heart lurched. It could happen to them. In fact, it was a wonder that they hadn't overturned any number of times on the winding mountain road they had just traveled.

They all piled out to see the damage for themselves.

"B'longs to Overland Stagecoach, like ours," Otis said. "Ain't nothin' I kin do but help out."

When they arrived at the overturned coach, its wheels were still spinning. Inside, the passengers had all tumbled to the roof of the coach. "Murder!" "Stop them hosses!" "Help!" some shouted. "Get us out of here!"

Otis ran to help the other driver rein the frightened horses under control while Uncle Franklin opened the door to help the passengers. One huge potbellied man lay atop all of the others.

Below him, a squashed traveler yelled, "Get that butterball off of me! Off, I beg!"

"I cain't budge!" the fat man said. "I truly cain't budge!"

The traveler below him planted his teeth in the calf of the fat man's leg.

"Call off your dog! Call him off!" screamed the portly man, then managed to scramble off the rest of them.

From somewhere under the pile, a woman screamed, "You're hurting my *limb!*"

"Tsk, tsk. What a scandal," Mrs. Fortran said. "All morning I've been expecting an overturn of our coach myself."

Finally the unfortunate passengers untangled themselves. Stepping out onto the Road, they walked about to "try their bodies" and found there was little harm done.

Suzannah let out a breath of relief, glad no one was hurt.

Otis and the driver of the overturned stage were already deciding how best to right the vehicle.

"Women and children out of our way now," Otis said. "If we men cain't push the coach over, we'll have to use the horses."

Charles was the only man who didn't offer to help. He swung back onto Lucky. "Guess I'll ride on."

Pauline looked stricken. "Oh, Charles, must you?"

"I need to see about our next inn." And with that he rode away without a backward glance.

That Charles! thought Suzannah. Everybody knew all the stops had been arranged ahead of time!

"Charles!" Uncle Franklin called after him. "Charles Herrington!"

But Charles, galloping on Lucky, was already well down the Road.

"You can't tell me Charles didn't hear your father," Suzannah muttered to Daniel.

Daniel shrugged. "There's nothing we can do. It's between them."

Pauline's eyes brimmed with tears, and Suzannah realized that more discussion would only make things worse for her sister. "I'm sorry, Pauline."

All in all, though, everyone seemed happier without Charles along. And Suzannah turned her attention to the efforts to right the overturned stagecoach.

"Since it's going to take a while to get that stagecoach right side up, why don't we stretch our legs?" Daniel said to Suzannah and Timmy. "Father, is that all right?"

Uncle Franklin nodded. "Sounds like a good idea to me, but stay on the Road."

"It feels good to get out," Suzannah said as the three of them set out. "And if we get hungry," she patted her traveling bag, "I have those strawberry jam sandwiches the last innkeeper's wife gave us. We can eat them for our mid-morning snack."

"Yum!" Timmy said, hurrying to keep up.

Beside the Road, a few bushes had already sent out spring buds, and the grasses were beginning to green up after the long winter. They stopped to peer into the forest. The filtered beams struck the new spring growth and set it aglow in a green-gold haze. Nearby, though, untouched snow lay deep and thick against shrubbery and tree trunks.

"Let's have a snowball fight!" cried Timmy.

They ventured into the woods only a few steps to get the soft snow which was just right for packing. Soon snowballs were flying.

"Got you, Daniel!" Suzannah shouted as one plastered his face, freezing his grin.

"And here's one for you!" He snapped a quick return and sent the snowball sailing through the air. She ducked, and it splatted harmlessly on the shoulder of her cloak.

They were having a fine time, wandering deeper and deeper into the forest, when Timmy said, "Look!"

Suzannah turned. Just behind her stood two bear cubs. Plump and round, they had bright button eyes and soft-as-down fur. She put out her hand and took a step toward them.

Curious, one of the cubs shuffled over to nose her traveling bag.

As if from nowhere, a huge black bear appeared out of the dark recesses of the forest. Rising up on its hind feet, the bear growled. Even in the shadows, Suzannah could see a row of sharp teeth and the long toenails extending from the front feet.

Daniel, who'd been gathering snow further away, caught sight of them. "The mother bear! Run!" he shouted.

But Suzannah stood rooted to the spot, her legs weak and heavy. Beside her, Timmy seemed just as stunned.

"Run!" Daniel urged again. "They smell the strawberry jam sandwiches! Leave your bag and run!"

The thought of parting with the gold coins jolted Suzannah into action. "Run, Timmy, run!" Traveling bag in hand, she ran with him for the Road.

Once she turned, almost tripping over a tree root, and saw the cubs still behind them and the huge mother bear in pursuit. Suddenly Suzannah knew just what to do. Still running wildly, she grabbed in her bag for the strawberry jam sandwiches, then pulled one out and hurled it at a cub.

The cub stopped to eat the sandwich, paper and all, and the other cub and mother bear stopped to join in.

Up ahead the forest thinned. "We're almost there!" she yelled. Looking back, she saw that the bears had finished the sandwich and were coming after them again.

Panting heavily, she reached into her bag for another sandwich. She threw it hard as she could, trying to get it behind them so they'd turn back.

"Head for the stagecoaches!" Daniel cried.

When they broke through the woods to the Road, Suzannah saw that the other stagecoach was upright and the passengers were boarding once more. "Bears!" she screamed. "Bears!"

She aimed another sandwich toward the mother bear, who was lumbering behind her.

Otis shouted, "Hurry! We're ready to ride!"

Glancing back as she ran, Suzannah saw that the mother bear had devoured the last sandwich and was fast closing the distance between them.

Suzannah grabbed for the last sandwich. It slipped from her hand back into the bag. She grabbed again, and this time she got it and threw with all her might. Then she turned and ran for her life.

They had just reached the stagecoach door when the bear broke out of the woods.

Uncle Franklin pulled them in and slammed the door. "Go . . . Otis . . . go!"

The stagecoach moved forward jerkily, and the three of them fell back in a jumble of arms and legs. "We made it!" Suzannah cried, pulling herself off the floor for one last look. The bears stood in the road, gazing after them.

"They're still groggy from hibernation," Uncle Franklin said. "And it's a good thing they are, too."

Suzannah nodded, settling down in her seat. "A good thing, all right. I couldn't have run another step."

Uncle Franklin's voice grew stern. "I thought I told the three of you to stay on the Road."

Suzannah scrunched back in her seat, feeling guilty. "I'm sorry—"

"We just stepped into the woods a little ways to get some snow for our snowball fight," Daniel explained.

"Wanting something where you're not supposed to be generally leads straight to trouble," Uncle Franklin said.

"We won't do it again," Daniel promised.

"I hope not, Son. I believe it was harder on us to see you running from those bears than it was on you."

Aunt Ruthie patted Uncle Franklin's arm. "All's well that ends well, dear."

"That might be," he replied, his jaw tightening. "But the fact is they didn't obey. Next time, the outcome might not be so good."

"The providence of God was surely watching over them," Aunt Ruthie said.

"But isn't it lucky that I thought of those jam sandwiches?" Suzannah asked, pleased that her fast thinking had saved them.

"But who put the idea in your head?" her uncle pressed.

Suzannah shrugged. To be honest, she hadn't given God a thought until now. Back in the forest, there hadn't even been time to pray!

Uncle Franklin said, "It won't hurt you to remember that God still has His say in things."

Suzannah nodded. Maybe God did help her. Maybe He even kept her coins safe. But she still kept her arms wrapped tight around her traveling bag—just in case.

CHAPTER 7

When they stopped early one afternoon for more repairs on the coach, Suzannah decided she must finally write to Jenny. Somehow she would get the letter posted without Charles's knowing.

Sitting in a window seat in the parlor of the inn, she wrote:

Almost to Indianapolis, Indiana

My dear friend, Jenny,

> *You must have guessed that I didn't know we were leaving Alexandria, or I would have bade you a tearful farewell. We've been traveling ever since, jolting along in a stagecoach on the National Road.*

> *People say the Road is as busy with "wheel traffic" as the Mississippi River is with boats, and I'm beginning to believe it. Some of the traffic, like stagecoaches and Conestoga wagons, hurries. Some, like farm carts, plods along. Part of the traffic goes at the*

*pace of a fine saddle horse, and part drags along as
slowly as a great flock of sheep balking and baaing
all the way. It's a hard journey, but it's an exciting adventure, too.*

*Once Cousin Daniel, Timmy (a new friend), and I
were chased by bears! We escaped by the skin of our
teeth—and with the help of some strawberry jam
sandwiches that I threw back to slow them down.*

*We've endured a blizzard, icy roads, and being
jounced until our bones ache. A few days ago we
spotted some black men lurking under a bridge near
the Road's edge. They were escaping from the South
to the Quaker village of Richmond here in Indiana.
We picked up a frontiersman, a real ruffian, several
stops ago, and he said blacks had no right "to take up
land and sech."*

*When Uncle Franklin told him that the Bible says
God made man in His own image and that meant
each of us, the fellow quieted a bit, but he said he
didn't "have much to do with God, either."*

*Just over the Ohio line in Richmond, we saw
Quakers in their dove-colored garments. The girls
and young women looked beautiful with snowy ker-
chiefs worn over their hair. A mantle of quiet lay over
the town. It was neat and clean, even though there
were mills, factories, and farms all around. The
Quakers are not allowed music or reading books,
though. Wouldn't you and I miss both?!*

*Now farther into Indiana, the Road is only sur-
faced here and there. Even so, there's an endless
stream of carts, stagecoaches, and carriages going
westward. What we see most, though, are the canvas-
topped wagons of settlers coming to farm the broad*

prairies. Some of them are "emigrants"—farmers who have worn out their soil and are moving on, hoping to find "greener pastures." They often bring cows, sheep, and pens of chickens along with them!

Yesterday we saw a cabin built on top of a wagon, fireplace and all! A window allowed the children to see out. Uncle Franklin joked that their barns and outhouses might still be following, "fetching up the rear" behind us on the Road.

The inns are so crowded that there are sometimes seven or eight women and their children sleeping together in one room. Jamie is having a fine time with so much to see and with so much attention.

Pauline is sketching the sights so we can always remember our adventure. Maybe she'll make you a copy of the sketch she made of me staring out the stagecoach window as we escaped the bears. (She drew me wide-eyed, and the mother bear with strawberry jam on her face. It's a comical picture, but it wasn't in the least funny when it happened!)

I miss you, my dear friend. I try to keep thoughts of you and Alexandria behind now, so it doesn't hurt so much. Never fear, though, I shall never forget you. I promise to write again, and trust you won't show the letters to anyone.

Your best friend still, I hope,

Suzannah

P.S. Interesting as all of this is, I miss going to school. You know how much I'd hoped to be a teacher like Aunt Ruthie was, but she says we are getting fine lessons in geography and human nature just traveling on the Road.

The Road ran right through the city of Indianapolis, passing the state capitol. The large pillars were of brick and stucco instead of marble, "modeled after the famous Parthenon in Athens, Greece," said Aunt Ruthie. She tried not to miss a single opportunity to "improve their minds."

"Bless my brain! I've driven by these parts many a time and not known thet!" Gabe confessed. "You'd make a scholar of me yit, Miz Colton, if I wasn't gittin' off the coach in Illinois."

Uncle Franklin patted his wife's hand and smiled proudly. "You're right about that. Ruthie has a way of making any outing a learning experience."

"Don't hold with book larnin'," said the frontiersman, who had found something to complain about ever since he had joined them. "Bad fer the head."

"What *do* you hold with?" Uncle Franklin seemed genuinely curious.

"Frontierin'," the man replied. "Soon's I get me enough money, I'm goin' up to the Oregon Territory."

"The Oregon Territory!"

"Yep. Ain't impossible now that Lewis and Clark been there. Ain't impossible a'tall."

"Don't give my husband and son any more ideas," said Aunt Ruthie. "As it is, they're middle-named Meriwether and have the itchy feet of explorers!"

"Named Meriwether . . . fer Lewis?" The grizzled fellow cocked his head and squinted at her.

Aunt Ruthie nodded. "Meriwether Lewis was a friend of the Colton family."

"Well, I'm goin' even if I ain't got Meriwether Lewis or William Clark in my name. From what I hear, plenty of wagons are settin' out fer Oregon this spring. Out there, they got fish as long as Indian canoes . . . apples as big as a baby's head . . . corn thet grows more n' ten feet tall . . . and, best of all, no winter!"

"I've also heard some fine things about the Oregon Territory," agreed Uncle Franklin. "I'd like to go there myself someday."

Aunt Ruthie darted a worried glance at him. "Independence, Missouri, is far enough for me, Franklin Meriwether Colton!"

Uncle Franklin patted her hand again. "Seems far enough to me, too, at this rate of travel."

Suzannah was glad when the frontiersman left the stagecoach. It was hard enough getting to Independence, Missouri, without putting thoughts of the Oregon Territory into Uncle Franklin's head. As it was, they had more important problems.

For one, Charles had ridden ahead to meet them in Terre Haute and was probably gambling away whatever money he had left. For another, ever since the bear chase Joad had been down on Timmy. Whenever he found a chance, he'd give the boy a well-aimed clout.

One day after their midday meal, Suzannah asked Timmy, "What's wrong between you and Joad now?"

He shrugged. "When my relatives paid my stagecoach fare, they said Joad had to take care of me."

"He has a strange way of doing it," Suzannah said. "Of course, it can't be much fun for him now, getting out and pulling the horses when they balk in the mud."

"Wonder if my relations in Vandalia, Illinois, are like him," Timmy said, looking scared.

So that's what was bothering him!

"Maybe Joad's just jealous that people like you," Suzannah put in, eager to relieve Timmy's mind. But the words were no more out of her mouth than she saw Joad approaching.

"You talkin' 'bout me?'"

"Why should we be?" she bluffed.

Checking to be sure his uncle was busy with the horses, Joad's eyes narrowed into slits, then he doubled his fists and hit Timmy in the face.

"Hey!" Timmy yelled, blood spurting from his nose.

"Stop that!" Daniel said. He pinned one of Joad's arms, while Suzannah grabbed the other.

"You leave him alone!" she yelled.

Hearing the noise, Otis Mout hurried over and spotted Timmy's bloody nose. "What's goin' on here, Joad?"

"Nothin'," Joad said, jerking himself free. "Jest plain nothin'."

"Then why's Tim's nose bleedin'?"

Suzannah couldn't stop herself. "He's always beating on Timmy . . . and Timmy has never done a mean thing to him! Never!"

Otis Mout grabbed Joad by the arm. "My patience is worn out with you, son or not. Tonight I'll fix it so you can't sit down comfortable fer a week."

At that moment, Uncle Franklin, who had been speaking with the innkeeper, arrived on the scene. "What's the trouble?" he asked, eyeing them suspiciously.

"Nothin' I cain't take keer of, Mr. Colton." Otis looked grim.

"I hope so," Uncle Franklin said. "I won't put up with bullies beating smaller children."

Subdued, they all climbed into the stagecoach and set off again. Aunt Ruthie finally stopped Timmy's nosebleed, but no matter how hard they tried to cheer him up, he didn't crack a single smile.

That night they stayed at Halfway Inn in Putnam County between Indianapolis and Terre Haute. When Joad and Otis Mout came in from the stables, Joad was walking stiffly and looked madder than ever.

Suzannah had been sitting on the front door stoop with Daniel and Timmy. "Appears he got a good licking, and I can't say I'm sorry," she observed.

"Me neither," Daniel said.

Timmy didn't say a word.

Usually the three of them explored their surroundings before dark, but that night Timmy stayed to himself. At suppertime they couldn't find him anywhere.

"We'd better hunt for him ourselves," she said. "No telling what his Uncle Otis would do."

Daniel thought for a moment. "Last I saw, he was wandering toward the stables. You suppose he'd take a horse and run off?"

"The way Joad treats him, I wouldn't be surprised," Suzannah replied. "We'd better go check!"

They hurried out to the stables, but no one had seen an eight-year-old boy.

"Anybody leave lately?" Daniel asked the stable boy.

"Nope," he said. "This time of night, most folks are comin' in."

They left the stables and scanned the darkening countryside. "It's too cold for Timmy to hide out in the woods,"

Suzannah said. "Besides, after our trouble with the bears, he wouldn't try that!"

They returned to the inn through the wagon yard, peering into the stagecoaches, buggies, and Conestoga wagons parked for the night. One of the Conestogas had come in shortly after their arrival, and the horses were still in harness tied to the post.

"I'm on me way home to Terre Haute," the wagoner had told Otis Mout. "Got rid of me load."

Suzannah brightened. "I'll bet Timmy heard that wagoner say he was moving on after supper." She frowned thoughtfully. "If I were unhappy and trying to get away from someone . . . I think I'd . . . hide in that wagon—there, *that* one—" She pointed to six mud-spattered bay horses, who stood drowsing in front of the big Conestoga wagon.

As Suzannah and Daniel neared the back of the canvas-topped freight wagon, Daniel called out, "Timmy? You in there?"

There was not a sound except for the whinny of a horse and the stamping of hooves.

"Tim—" Suzannah called again. "If you're in there, please say so. We just want to hel—"

From inside the wagon came Timmy's voice in a poor imitation of Otis Mout. "Get along, boys! Get along!" He slapped the reins over the horses' backs, and they started off at a brisk trot.

"Wait, Timmy!" Suzannah cried, running after the wagon. "Wait!"

"Get along, boys!" Timmy sounded desperate now, flailing the reins as if his life depended on it.

"Whoa, boys!" Daniel yelled.

"Stop the horses!" Suzannah called to Daniel.

"That's exactly what I'm trying to do! Whoa, boys!" But nothing either of them yelled did any good.

Running at full speed, Daniel caught hold of the tailgate and finally hoisted himself up and over and into the wagon.

"Help me up!" Suzannah grasped the back of the wagon, trying to stay clear of the huge wheels, and hung on as it jolted along through the courtyard and out toward the main road. "Daniel, help!"

Just as she got one foot on the tailgate, Daniel grabbed her hand and pulled hard. It felt as if her arm would come loose from its socket. Then the wagon hit a deep rut and bounced her up into the moving wagon, blue skirt flying.

The horses ran faster and faster. When Suzannah finally struggled to a sitting position, she could see why.

Timmy had toppled off the driver's seat and had lost the reins, giving the horses their head, while the wagon pitched and swayed like a sailing boat caught in a storm.

Gripping the wooden slats of the wagon, she and Daniel slowly made their way to the front, where Timmy clung to the back of the driver's seat. "I . . . I was only thinking of hiding and riding away with the wagoner," he cried, "and then *you* had to come!"

"Yeah, we *had* to come!" Suzannah replied. "Did you think we'd let you disappear without a worry?"

"Guess I didn't think about that," Timmy said. "But after Joad got that licking, I knew he'd be meaner than ever to me."

"Maybe," she said. "But maybe not. We'll talk about it later!"

Holding onto the driver's seat, Suzannah stuck her head out the opening of the white canvas. The tangled reins whipped about, but she couldn't reach them. "Whoa, boys!" she shouted. "Whoa!"

Beside her, Daniel joined in. "Whoa, boys!" But it appeared that the horses were making the most of a good run with an empty wagon.

In the growing darkness, she could just make out a sign that read "Terre Haute," but she guessed that the horses didn't have to read it or the passing milepost to know where they were going. They were on their way home!

CHAPTER 8

A full moon lit the night sky and poured a path of light down the middle of the National Road. The horses pulling the freight wagon with the Colton cousins and Timmy aboard raced on. Ahead was a lantern-lit buggy and a stage-coach, but the runaway team didn't move over for either of them.

"Runaway team!" Suzannah, Daniel, and Timmy shouted through the opening in the white canvas. "Runaway team!" The buggy and stagecoach scattered like startled hens to the side of the Road, the drivers yelling and shaking their fists.

"Whoa, boys!" Daniel and Timmy called out again and again. "Whoa, boys!"

"They're not even tired!" Suzannah cried, fear churning in her stomach. "What'll we do now?"

"Looks like we'll have to ride it out!" shouted Daniel above the roar of the pounding hooves. "That is, unless we can jump clear of the wagon!"

Suzannah eyed the passing roadway with alarm. "We'd be sure to break something! And Timmy—"

"Then the only other hope is to catch those reins!"

"You'll have to do it, Daniel! You're the only one of us who's ever driven horses!"

Unfortunately, he'd only driven two old nags to make shop deliveries in Georgetown, but now was no time to say so. Daniel drew a deep breath. "Then you two hold on to me, and I'll lean out as far as I can!"

Just then, the wagon pitched through rut after bone-jarring rut. "Be careful!" Suzannah exclaimed.

Daniel nodded, but looked determined. "Here, take hold of the back of my pants, Timmy. And, Suzannah, you grip my shoulders."

He settled into the driver's seat, and they latched on to him, bracing themselves.

In the moonlight, the reins danced about wildly just out of reach. For a very long time, it seemed, they whipped everywhere but in his direction, slapping the horses and urging them on. Then suddenly one of the reins flew toward the canvas opening, and Daniel leaned forward and grabbed it.

"Got one!" He handed it to Suzannah. "Hold this . . . but don't pull on it!"

She took the rein in one hand and a handful of Daniel's shirt in the other. "I think it belongs to the front left horse!" she told him.

"I know! If we can just get control of the team, they might trot on home without doing themselves any damage!" Again Daniel leaned way out to grab for the flying strips of leather.

After a long while, the reins lashed toward him. Suzannah held onto Daniel with all of her might as he reached out as far as he dared. After three tries he caught another one. "Got it!" He held it up triumphantly.

"Front right horse," Suzannah said.

Daniel sat down and braced himself. "Let me try working those reins on the horses."

She handed them over.

Suddenly she knew what she could do. She could pray. *If it's true Thou dost really help people in trouble, please, Lord, I'm asking now! We didn't mean to steal these horses or the wagon, Lord . . . and Timmy didn't, either. He was just hiding, and we wanted to help—*

"Whoa, boys!" Daniel called out again. "Whoa!"

Little by little the two lead horses slowed, forcing the others to slacken their pace too. Not any too soon either. At the next milepost the Road turned into a quagmire. The horses had slowed just enough to avoid running into it. As it was, just before they stopped, their hooves made an awful sucking sound as they pulled them from the mud.

"Whew!" Suzannah said. "They could have broken their legs, running into that mud. We'd better get them off the road."

Slowly Daniel maneuvered the horses and wagon onto the higher ground along the roadside, and the three of them peered ahead into the distance. As far as they could see westward, the National Road looked like a slimy bog surrounded by thick forest. They sat in silence, wondering what to do next while the horses snorted and stamped, their breath white puffs in the cold night air.

"I don't think it's a good idea to go on tonight," Suzannah said finally. "We can't see where we're going, and the horses are tired."

"I guess you know we're already in plenty of trouble," Daniel said. He jumped out to rub down the team, wiping the flecks of lather from their coats with an old rag he had found in the wagon. "That drover's going to be mad as anything that we took his wagon. Not to mention my dad! We could be taken for horse thieves!"

"I know. But maybe we could drive on to Terre Haute . . . find Charles, and wait for the others."

"Maybe," Daniel said. "When it's daylight, I suppose we could drive them around the edge of the mire."

"What'll we d—do 'til then?" asked Timmy in a high, quavery voice.

"Guess we'll just have to sleep in the wagon," Suzannah said firmly, determined not to let Timmy think she was afraid. It wouldn't do to frighten him any more than he already was.

Suzannah got out of the wagon. Once she was on solid ground, her body quivered as if she were still riding. It was one thing to ride in a stagecoach, but quite another to ride in an empty Conestoga with a runaway team.

"I don't care if I never see another wagon as long as I live!" she announced.

"Then how do you plan to get to Terre Haute?" Daniel asked.

Just then they heard the sound of approaching riders coming down the Road.

"There's my wagon!" someone shouted. "If I get my hands on those kids—"

"We'd better run!" Suzannah whispered.

"Quick! The woods—"

Daniel led the way. Hidden by the Conestoga, they crept quietly behind a thick stand of pine trees.

The little group of riders pulled to a halt in front of the wagon and dismounted.

"Looks like the hosses are plumb wore out, but 'pears to be no damage done," said the wagoner, running a practiced hand over the sweaty flanks. "Figgered those young'uns would kill 'em runnin' into that bog."

"They're winded. Don't reckon these horses will be goin' anywhere tonight," said another.

"Nope. I'll just sleep right here in my wagon. Then we kin git us an early start come mornin'."

From their hiding place in the woods, Suzannah, Daniel, and Timmy watched as the wagoner climbed into the wagon to settle down for the night while his companions mounted up and turned their horses back toward Halfway Inn.

Once they were gone, the night and the forest seemed to close in. Suzannah remembered running from the bears in Ohio. As it was, she could already hear distant hooting and howling, and she shivered. "It's too cold to sleep here in the forest," she whispered. "Wasn't there a dirt road just a ways back?"

"I think so," Daniel replied. "Could be someone has a place there, and we could sleep in a shed." He stopped to get his bearings. "It should be to the right—"

They made their way slowly along the edge of the forest, ducking behind the trees when another group of riders rode by on the Road.

It was slow going, but finally they found the dirt road. Here the woods were so thick that the moonlight barely filtered through. A light breeze rustled the papery thin leaves and sent chilly fingers down their spines.

No sooner had they started up the road than Suzannah tripped over a tree root and fell headlong, almost crying out. She was followed by Timmy, when he stumbled into a rut and hurt his knee. That was enough for Timmy to finally burst into tears.

"Let's hold hands," Suzannah suggested when they got him quiet. "Timmy in the middle."

The small boy squeezed their hands tightly while they moved ahead, feeling their way through the woods, until at last the road turned off into a small clearing. In the bright moonlight they could see not only a cabin but a barn.

Remembering the snug stable that had sheltered her and Daniel from the blizzard in the mountains, Suzannah's steps quickened.

Timmy stopped when they reached the barn door. "What if there's owls inside?"

"Owls won't hurt you," Daniel said. "Come on."

"Just stay close to us. We'll take care of you." Knowing that Timmy was depending on them gave Suzannah courage she didn't really feel.

Inside the barn door they paused, waiting until their eyes became adjusted to the darker interior. There were moos and an occasional neigh from the occupants inside, whose bedtime had been disturbed.

A shaft of moonlight through the open door revealed an empty stall between the cows and two horses. It wasn't as soft as a bed, but there was clean straw, and the instant Suzannah laid her head down, she was asleep.

"Alors! Qu'est-ce que c'est?"

From somewhere far away Suzannah could hear a deep voice, strangely accented. Coming awake, she opened one eye, then the other.

The first thing she saw was a great red beard! The beard was attached to a towering figure, looming above her like a mountain. Feet spread and hands on his hips, the "mountain" was dressed in a red fox hat and patched leather cape.

She sat bolt upright and stared at the man.

"Aimee! Viens!" he cried again, then launched into a long speech. She couldn't understand a single word he was saying.

Beside her, Timmy and Daniel were just as bewildered. "He's speaking some kind of French, I think," whispered Daniel, "but it doesn't sound much like the French I used to hear when I made deliveries to that restaurant in Georgetown."

Suzannah got to her feet, grateful that her traveling bag hadn't been stolen while she slept. She brushed the straw from her cloak. "Look, mister," she began, fumbling for her pouch of gold coins, "we were just tired and needed a place to sleep for the night. We didn't do any harm or take any-thing—"

"Aimee!" he bellowed again. "Nos enfants ne parlent pas Français!"

Suzannah's heart sank and she shoved the pouch deeper into the bag. She wasn't getting anywhere. Maybe Daniel could think of something.

"What's he sayin'?" Timmy wanted to know.

Suzannah shook her head. "I don't know. Gabe said lots of French trappers lived around here ages ago. Maybe he's gone crazy from being alone. Let's get out of here—"

Daniel held up his hand. "Wait a minute. He doesn't seem mad." He listened, trying to make out the strange phrases. "It sounds like he thinks we're . . . his children!"

Suzannah swallowed hard. This whole thing was getting stranger by the minute. Still, he deserved something for his trouble. Drawing out the little pouch again, she gave him a coin from her change purse.

"For the use of your barn." She folded her hands and tucked them under her face in the gesture of sleep, then pointed to the straw-filled stall.

He bit down on the coin with stained teeth. Giving a small nod, he put the coin into his pocket and looked at her and the boys again.

"Thank you, again," she said, starting for the door.

"Attendez! Attendez!" He grabbed her arm. "Aimee!" he bellowed again. "Viens vite! Les enfants veulent se sauver."

Suzannah froze. Whoever Amy was, she must be deaf, she thought, wondering why the whole countryside hadn't rushed to see what the excitement was about.

The only answer, however, was a moo from the cow in a nearby stall, and an answering neigh.

The man loosened his grip and Suzannah stepped back. "It's time we were on our way."

"Manger?" The man's bloodshot eyes widened. "Aha!" He made eating motions. "Manger! Aimee! Les enfants ont faim!"

"I think he's telling someone we're hungry," Daniel said.

Suzannah's stomach growled at the thought. "Eat?" she asked the man. "We haven't eaten since yesterday."

He grinned. "Venez avec moi." He spoke on rapidly and the next thing they knew, he was leading them to his log cabin. "Aimee!" he called ahead.

"Amy must be his wife," guessed Daniel. "Maybe she can give us something to eat."

A weathered wagon stood under the trees near the front door. "Pour quand je vais a Terre Haute," he said.

Suzannah nodded, though all she understood was Terre Haute, the next big town west. She guessed he must use the wagon to go there.

"Terre Haute?" He pointed to the three of them.

They all nodded, then Suzannah wished they hadn't.

Inside the dark cabin the windows were covered with oiled paper instead of glass. Dried animal skins hung on the chinked log walls. The man's bed was a platform built on poles and covered by a buffalo robe. On the dirt floor lay a huge bearskin, its black beady eyes staring up at them.

"Appears he's a trapper all right," Suzannah said.

"Looks like it," Daniel replied uneasily.

The cabin smelled of freshly baked bread. In fact, a loaf of it was cooling on top of the black iron stove that stood in the middle of the log room.

"Attendez," he said to the three of them. Grabbing a thick rag, he opened the oven door and pulled out another loaf. He held up two fingers. "Deux pains aujourd'hui."

"He made two loaves of bread today," Daniel translated.

"Aimee!" he called over his shoulder.

But no one came.

"Asseyez-vous." He motioned them toward the rough wooden benches alongside the plank table. They sat. Wooden dishes and bits of old food lay scattered over the stained plank.

After a while, the man poured milk into tin cups and added a round of butter for their bread. "Mangez bien!"

Daniel said grace, and Suzannah remembered: "I will fear no evil, for thou art with me." The words from the Psalm were soothing.

The prayer seemed to unsettle the trapper, though, for he was frowning as he cut large slices of bread with a huge carving knife. The blade seemed especially sharp, and Suzannah and Daniel exchanged worried looks.

"Mangez bien," he said again, indicating that they were to eat.

The warm bread and butter was so delicious that they downed the entire loaf without saying another word, then looked up at him guiltily.

He grinned at them with pleasure. "Bien."

"He's pleased we ate well," Daniel said.

Suzannah felt an urge to give the trapper another small coin from her change purse. "Thank you for the food," she said, handing it over. "Now we really must go."

They stood up, and the giant of a man beamed with pleasure. "Ah, Aimee—"

Suzannah was astonished to see the trapper hold his arm lovingly around the empty space beside him.

"It's time to go!" she whispered to Daniel and Timmy, edging toward the door.

The boys were right behind her, and when they reached the safety of the outdoors, they raced for the dirt road, expecting the man to be close on their heels. But there was no sound of pounding footsteps or shouts.

"He's probably still talking to the invisible Amy," sighed Suzannah, when they stopped at last to catch their breath. "I do feel sorry for him. He seems so lonely. But I'm glad we got away when we did."

"Yes! But he might still change his mind and come for us in his wagon!" yelled Daniel, taking off again down the dirt road.

With that thought in mind, they raced through the woods for the Road.

CHAPTER 9

Coming onto the National Road in full daylight, Suzannah saw that the traffic had picked up from the night before. Stagecoaches bound for Terre Haute and points west, farm wagons piled with homesteading supplies, and riders galloping by kept the pace lively.

She glanced behind her down the dirt lane. "No sign of the trapper."

"No sign of the Conestoga we made off with, either." Daniel had quickly scanned the area for the sail-like canvas. "But I think I'd rather *walk* to Terre Haute anyway," he said, breaking into a big grin.

"I'm sorry I got us in trouble," Timmy said, ducking his head and kicking a boot against the hardening mud. "It's all my fault that we're lost way out here."

Daniel tousled Timmy's hair. "Father always says it's no use to cry over spilt milk. Besides, I'm not worried."

"You're not?" Timmy looked over at him with awe. "What about you, Suzannah?"

She shrugged. "Oh, I figure our stagecoach will come along and spot us," she said with confidence. "If not, we'll catch up with them in Terre Haute."

"What if . . . we can't find them?"

Suzannah thought about the gold coins in her traveling bag and squeezed it gratefully under her arm. "I have my ways. Don't worry."

"You're both pretty brave," Timmy said. "I'm glad you're not angry with me."

"There wasn't time to be angry," Suzannah said. "And now it's too late."

Timmy looked relieved.

With the sun warm on their backs, they walked west alongside the Road, watching for ruts and stumps to avoid. Every so often, they glanced back to be sure the trapper's wagon was not rumbling behind them. "I've heard of people like him, but I never expected to see one," Daniel said. "He did beat all."

"I wonder what his Amy looks like," Suzannah said. "She's probably very beautiful to him."

"I had an invisible friend once . . . when I was little," Timmy said in a small voice.

"Some sprigs do when they're lonely, so I've heard," Daniel said, " 'specially if they don't have any brothers or sisters . . . or cousins." He gave Suzannah a big grin.

Timmy nodded. After a moment, he said, "Guess I'll tell you. When I hid in that Conestoga, I was planning to go to Vandalia and spy around to see what my aunt and cousins

were like. If they were like Joad, I wasn't going to stay. I—
I'd rather be alone . . . like that trapper."

"You mean you'd want to be a hermit?" Suzannah asked
in alarm.

He shook his head. "I don't think so . . . now. But I wish
you and Daniel . . . and your Aunt Ruthie and Uncle
Franklin . . . were my family."

Suzannah would have hugged him if she hadn't been
afraid it would embarrass him. Instead, she said, "Don't you
worry, Timmy. If it doesn't work out, we'll take care of—"

Daniel cut her off. "You know we can't make promises
like that."

"Then what *can* we do?" she asked, aggravated.

"Pray," Daniel said. "We can pray."

She remembered her prayer on the runaway wagon and
knew he was right. "Then I will. I'm going to pray like anything for you, Timmy."

"Well—" He seemed confused. "Just so I have a real
friend."

"But you can," Suzannah replied. "You can have the same
Friend I have inside . . . He's invisible, but He's not like
Amy. He's *real*."

Timmy squinted at her. "What do you mean?"

Suzannah smiled. "You said you went to church with your
family, so I thought you knew. But . . . well, some people
think they're Christians just because they're good and go to
church. But that's not all of it. You have to have Jesus in your
heart, too."

"Do *you*?"

Suzannah nodded. "I do now, but I didn't always. Then one day when I felt as awful as awful could be, I said, 'Please come into my heart, Lord Jesus.' "

"You mean you asked . . . in church?" Timmy asked.

Suzannah shook her head. "No, right in my bedroom."

"What happened then?"

"Before long I stopped feeling awful and felt joyous . . . you know, glad in my heart. Now Jesus is my Friend, Someone I can always talk to, no matter what."

"But not like Amy?" Timmy asked.

"Not like Amy. Jesus is real," Suzannah promised. "He's God's Son, His only Son. If you pray and listen, He tells you what to do."

Timmy glanced at Daniel. "Is He in your heart?"

Daniel nodded. "He sure is!"

"Your mother and father, too?"

Daniel nodded. "Yes, they're believers . . . and so is Pauline. But we're not perfect. Only the Lord is."

"How does He answer you when you talk to Him?"

Suzannah replied, "Last night when the horses were running so hard, I prayed for help, and then Daniel caught the reins, and the horses slowed just before that swampy stretch of Road. But—" She blushed. "I didn't even remember to thank Him before I fell asleep!"

She thought back. "Then, when Daniel blessed the food in the trapper's cabin, the Lord made me more peaceful and I wasn't as scared." Her voice grew softer. "You know, I used to think that I got myself out of that blizzard and got us away from that bear, but I think God helped us then too." She remembered the frantic carriage chase from her house in Alexandria. "And lots of other times." She paused. "But we're not supposed to pray just when we need help, but *all* the time—" Suzannah's voice trailed away. Lately she sure hadn't acted as if she believed that. "I guess I don't always remember that I belong to God—"

There was a long silence as the three walked along, thinking deep thoughts. Then Timmy said, "I'd like to belong to Him too."

Amazed at what she had heard, Suzannah stopped walking and looked at Timmy.

Daniel spoke up. "It's easy. Just ask Him to forgive you and tell Him you want Him to come into your heart to live. You don't even have to wait for Sunday."

"Then I want to do it right now." Right there on the Road, Timmy bowed his head. "Jesus, forgive all of my badness. And please come live in my heart. I want Thee to be my Friend, and I want to belong to Thee."

When they walked on, Suzannah felt full of wonder, just like she had the day she gave her heart to Jesus. Even the mud and stumps on the roadside looked different somehow. With the bright blue sky above and the forest all around, the world seemed a beautiful place—a holy place. *I thank Thee, Lord, for saving Timmy,* she prayed. *Please take care of him . . . and help me remember that Thou art the One who answers my prayers and watches over me . . . and that I'm not so smart, after all!*

Later they came upon a drover trying to move a herd of pigs through the mud. "*Move,* you porkers!" he shouted. "Move on!" He poked the balky pigs with a stick while they rolled in the mud, holding up the traffic.

Nearby, a Conestoga driver hung out of his wagon and bellowed, "Git along! Git those hogs along!"

A farmer, waiting in his wagon, shook his fist. "We ain't got all day!" And just ahead, a stagecoach had tried to go around on the shoulder of the Road, and one of the horses had thrown a shoe. Ten or twelve stagecoaches and wagons waited on the other side of the swampy stretch, and even more waited to roll westward.

Suzannah looked carefully at the vehicles lining the Road as far as she could see. "Let's keep a sharp eye out for our coach. They've surely had breakfast by now and will be along soon."

"There's a green coach like ours!" Timmy yelled. At that moment a stagecoach door burst open and out jumped Uncle Franklin. He waved and ran toward them, Aunt Ruthie and Pauline close behind.

"We've been hoping and praying we'd find you along the Road!" He caught Suzannah and Daniel in a mighty hug.

"It was all my fault," Timmy said, hanging his head.

Uncle Franklin gave Timmy a hug that lifted him off the ground. "No sense in worrying about whose fault it was. The main thing is that you're safe."

Then Pauline and Aunt Ruthie were hugging all three of them. "Where were you? What happened?"

"It's a long story," Suzannah said, then told them everything except the part about Timmy's prayer, since that wasn't hers to tell.

When they neared the coach, Otis nodded, but kept his seat, and Joad glowered.

Otis said to Timmy, "Joad will keep his hands off ye from now on. Ye can count on thet."

Timmy smiled a little. "Thank you, Uncle Otis."

Joad looked away grimly.

Inside the coach, Gabe Multon, Mrs. Fortran, and Jamie beamed at them, and Suzannah and Daniel had to explain their adventure all over again.

Pauline told them, "Uncle Franklin, Mr. Multon, and Mr. Mout went out riding after you, and came back hoarse from shouting."

"You must have been the second group of riders we heard," Suzannah said, "but we hid in the trees. We didn't know it was you."

"No doubt the wind was blowing in the wrong direction for ye to make out the voices," Gabe said.

At long last the pigs were all herded through the quagmire. As the coach started forward along the edge of the Road, Aunt Ruthie settled back against her seat. "Well, all's well that ends well, and that's what's important now. I only feel sorry for that old trapper with no one to love."

"When I drove my peddlin' wagon in these parts, I saw lots of emigrants like thet," said Gabe thoughtfully. "After they settled Pennsylvania, they filled Ohio. Next, they moved on into Indiana to build their homes and plant their fields. They cling to this Road like mosquitoes cling to a bald fella's head."

Pauline studied a sketch she had just finished. "Are many of the emigrants lonely?"

"Yep. Most of 'em, I reckon. Leastways, the ones like me . . . without no families."

Suzannah had never thought much about being lonely. Even after her parents died, she'd had Pauline, Jamie, Aunt Ruthie, Uncle Franklin, and Daniel—and, of course, Charles, who wasn't much of a blessing.

As they neared Terre Haute, Pauline seemed agitated. She kept patting her hair and smoothing her rumpled gray traveling dress.

"I can't wait to see Charles," she said. "I'm sure he'll have things in order for us at Prairie House. After all those wagon stops, we'll sleep in a civilized hotel for a change."

I hope she's right about Charles, Suzannah thought.

When they stopped for lunch, they found pork chops the main item on the menu. "I hope it's not those pigs we saw rolling in the quagmire," Aunt Ruthie said.

Suzannah pushed the slices of pork to the rim of her plate. "Yuck!" she choked. She filled up on carrots, cornbread, and mashed potatoes instead.

Just as they were taking the last bites of their apple cobbler, Mrs. Fortran cried out in alarm. "My gold brooch . . . it's missing!"

They searched her chair, under the table, and all around the wide plank floor, feeling in all the crevices. While she was on her knees, Suzannah glanced up just in time to see Joad Mout watching them from the doorway. He was smiling, which made her suspicious.

When it was time to board the stagecoach once more, Mrs. Fortran still hadn't found her brooch. She gave the innkeeper her name and the address of her family in Vandalia in case it was found. "My mother gave it to me," she said, near tears. "It's very precious to me."

"The pin might be in the stagecoach," Uncle Franklin comforted her. "Or it could have fallen off when we walked to the inn. We'll make a thorough search."

Daniel whispered to Suzannah, "And might be Joad grabbed it when he helped Mrs. Fortran down from the coach."

She thought back. "You're right. He sure took his time helping her out."

As they walked outside, everyone searched for the brooch in the gravel driveway. Otis Mout and Joad had reached the coach, with Timmy right behind them, when Suzannah looked up. Just as Joad climbed up into the driver's box, the gold brooch tumbled out of his pocket.

Timmy picked it up. "Here it is, Mrs. Fortran! Here's your brooch!"

Mrs. Fortran accepted the pin from him and clasped it to her heart. "I can never thank you enough for finding it, Timmy. Never! You deserve a nice reward." She opened her handbag and took out her coin purse.

"Thank you, ma'am," he replied politely. "But I couldn't take it."

"But why ever not?"

"I couldn't because—"

Suzannah held her breath. Now was his chance. Would he tell on Joad?

"Why not?" Mrs. Fortran repeated, holding out a generous coin.

Timmy looked up at Joad, then back to Mrs. Fortran. "Because you're a nice lady and . . . I'm glad to help."

Oh, Timmy! Suzannah thought proudly. He was already listening to the Lord better than she did. Instead of making trouble, he was setting a good example for Joad and for the rest of them too.

Aunt Ruthie hugged Timmy, and Uncle Franklin gave him a proud pat on the back.

"I'd like to sketch a picture of you, Timmy," Pauline said. "Just at that special moment when you gave the brooch to

Mrs. Fortran. I have it all fixed in my head. Would you mind?"

"I guess not," he replied, his eyes shining.

Joad stared straight ahead.

He might never change, Suzannah thought, but he couldn't say he hadn't seen a good example of how to forgive!

———◆◆◆———

Terre Haute, a French named city, stood on a high bluff on the east bank of the Wabash River. As they rode into town, it felt as if they were finally in the West, even though it was only the far west of Indiana.

Pauline said again, "I can't wait to see Charles!"

I hope she won't be disappointed! Suzannah thought.

When they arrived at the red brick, four-story Prairie House Hotel, however, there was no sign of Charles. Worse, the desk clerk said, "We sent that card shark packing. You'll probably find him at the downtown hotel if not out on the Wabash, gambling on a riverboat. Been some Easterners asking about him too. I take it one fellow means him no good."

Suzannah couldn't help wondering if it was the same hawk-nosed man who had stopped their coach just out of Alexandria. And when Pauline burst into tears, all Suzannah could do was pat her hand and say, "Don't worry. He'll be all right."

"Yes, he always is, isn't he?" Pauline choked back a sob.

"Let's head for the hotel in town," Uncle Franklin suggested. "Maybe he's waiting for us there."

But there was no Charles.

"You Mrs. Herrington?" the hotel clerk asked Pauline.

"Yes . . . yes, I am," she replied, brightening.

"Your husband left this letter for you."

She tore open the envelope. Reading the letter, Pauline turned pale. "He's . . . gone on to Vandalia. Says he'll meet us there at the hotel."

They all stared at each other, stunned.

Suzannah guessed he knew the hawk-nosed man was after him. Charles was probably not only gambling, but still on the run.

"Well, there's nothing more we can do tonight. So let's get settled in our rooms," Uncle Franklin said in his most practical voice. "We'll all feel better after supper. Problems never seem quite as bad on a full stomach."

When they walked along the Wabash River after supper, Suzannah was glad that there were no showboats among those at the landing to remind them of Charles and his infernal gambling.

———◆◆◆———

The next day they crossed the Wabash River. A short distance to the south, the river marked the Indiana-Illinois border, then flowed into the mighty Ohio on its way to the Mississippi. Ten miles after their stagecoach crossed the Wabash River bridge, they were in Illinois themselves.

"Almost to Vandalia?" Timmy asked, a little worried.

"Oh, not yit, sonny," Gabe answered. "We've got a few more days of hard travelin'."

This was a good time to pray for Timmy again, Suzannah thought. He seemed to dread meeting his new family. She leaned her head back against the seat and closed her eyes for a moment. *Please Lord, help Timothy.*

Mrs. Fortran looked worried too. "The countryside seems a bit wilder."

Unfortunately, the same was true of the Road. When they came to more and more quagmires, Otis and Joad had to get out to chop trees and widen the shoulder so they could drive on the higher ground. For days they bounced and jounced along.

At one stagecoach stop, they picked up an Illinois man who chewed tobacco and spit out the window at every chance. He also spoke endlessly, but his words were so slurred that they could scarcely understand him, except for an occasional, "Wal now, stranger."

When he got off at the next stop, Mrs. Fortran said, "I do hope my son hasn't become like that! He wasn't educated to such speech . . . or frontier ways."

Timmy had been eyeing the man with concern too. Suzannah knew what he was thinking. What if his new family turned out to be like him? *Lord*, Suzannah prayed, *please don't let them be like Joad and Otis . . . or the Illinois man!*

Gabe Multon left the stagecoach at the last stop before Vandalia. They all bade him a sad farewell while a fresh team of horses was being attached to the coach.

"If I can't find my kinfolk here, maybe I'll see you in Independence. Always been itchin' to go to the far west."

"We hope you do!" Suzannah called back through the open window. "Thank you for telling us about the Road!"

The stagecoach finally arrived in Vandalia, Illinois, which everyone found disappointing for a former state capital. Vandalia sat on the west bank of the Kaskaskia River, but the town had no marbled statehouse or other fine buildings. Instead, there was only an ordinary brick building that was now the courthouse.

Mrs. Fortran said, "Must be the government took the grandeur with them when they moved to Springfield." She squared her shoulders. "Well, I am determined to like it."

Timmy scarcely glanced at the buildings, and Suzannah prayed again for his life in this town.

When they pulled up at the stagecoach stop, Otis Mout handed down Mrs. Fortran into the hands of her son, who wore a suit and black bow tie. He looked quite respectable, Suzannah thought, as did his children. His wife also appeared to be a proper lady, the type who might occasionally say "Tsk, tsk" herself.

"Welcome, Mother," her son said, and they all hugged her warmly.

It was Timmy's turn. He stepped reluctantly from the coach, gave Suzannah a woebegone look, then darted anxious glances all around.

A shy woman with three little girls stepped forward. "Why . . . you must be Timmy," she said in a sweet voice. "You look just like your father did when he was little." She gave him a fond hug. "We're so pleased you're coming to live with us."

Her neatly bearded husband lifted Timmy's trunk down from the top of the stagecoach, then shook his hand. "It's about time we had another man around the house, son. I've been outnumbered far too long."

Timmy beamed up at him, then back at Suzannah and the others in the coach. "Thank you all . . . for everythin'," he said.

His aunt added, "And we thank you for your kindness to Timmy too."

Pauline handed Timmy the sketch she had made. "So you'll remember we're keeping you in our prayers."

He blinked hard as he took it, and his lips quivered a little. "Thank you, Pauline." He looked around for Suzannah and Daniel and gave them a happy smile. "I'll never forget you—"

As the stagecoach lurched forward, Suzannah and Daniel hung out the window, calling farewells to Timmy and Mrs. Fortran for as long as they could see them.

Suzannah felt as if she would burst with happiness. *Oh, Lord, I thank Thee for taking care of Mrs. Fortran, even though I forgot to pray for her. And I thank Thee for Timmy's new family. They're not a thing like Joad and Otis . . . or the Illinois man!*

CHAPTER 10

Suzannah jumped off the ferryboat onto the St. Louis levee, and the queen city of the Mississippi Valley unfolded before her.

"Look at that!" she called to Daniel.

St. Louis was a sight to behold—the noise, the people, the whole raucous city. There was a tannery, a foundry, a brewery, an ironworks, and a repair yard full of huge steamboats. There was a four-story hospital, a new courthouse, and the best hotels in the West.

As they rode along in another carriage to their hotel, Suzannah was surprised to hear familiar songs drifting from the taverns. She had always liked "Buffalo Gals." But from another doorway she heard the song she knew by heart— "Oh, Suzannah."

Daniel laughed. "Guess they know you're here!"

She made a face, then grinned back.

Pauline seemed anxious to see Charles despite everything. And for her sister's sake, Suzannah was pleased when he turned up at last, wearing a fine new suit and hat.

After he had kissed Pauline and Jamie, Charles turned to Suzannah. "Well, little sister-in-law, you're looking fit as always."

She guessed he was just trying to say something nice to avoid trouble, but she wasn't going to let him get away with it. "And you look like a riverboat gambler!"

"Suzannah!" Pauline gasped.

"Pauline, if you didn't put up with his gambling, maybe he'd quit!" Suzannah added while she was at it.

Charles ignored both of them and turned to the others with a gracious charm that made Suzannah sick to her stomach. "We'll have a fine supper tonight here at the hotel," he said. "It's such a relief to be among civilized people again."

Suzannah guessed from the look on Uncle Franklin's face that he'd have words with Charles when he could find him alone.

But Charles continued to act as if he hadn't done anything wrong. And true to his promise, they ate the best supper they'd had since they left home.

———◆◆———

It wasn't until the next afternoon that Suzannah had another chance to write to Jenny.

St. Louis, Missouri

My dearest friend, Jenny,

We are finally west of the Mississippi River—and what a journey it's been! After Indianapolis, the Road was no longer paved, and our stagecoach had to slip and slide through one quagmire after another.

After Vandalia, Illinois, the Road stopped. As Daniel said, "It surrendered to the wilderness!"

Uncle Franklin hired our driver to go on to the Mississippi River. Often there was nothing more than a trail. Where bridges should have been, only great tree trunks lay across the hollows. Driving over them, we jolted so that it nearly knocked our teeth loose.

Yesterday we bade our driver and his troublemaking son, Joad, farewell, then crossed the great Mississippi River on one of the ferryboats. We were packed in on the ferry with farm wagons, carts, and smelly livestock—and were more than glad to get off. What a change it was from the wooded shores of Illinois to the city of St. Louis!

I am looking out now from my hotel window and wish you were here to see the sights. St. Louis is such a big and busy place. I can see the Mississippi River and the boats on it from our hotel window. Yesterday we went for a stroll and saw rafts, canoes, pirogues, barges, skiffs, broadhorns, keelboats, and even a Daguerreotype flatboat from which they photograph people and places. Uncle Franklin says, "There's anything that can float downriver, and anything that can be pulled, pushed, poled, rowed, or sailed upstream!"

Pauline has been sketching the sights—settlers bound for Oregon and California, traders passing on their way to the Santa Fe Trail, rough trappers bringing their furs here from the mountains—some with beards nearly down to their knees! They wear buckskins fringed like those of the Indians and are glad to be told, "I took ye fer an Injun!"

Jamie has been "good as gold" through the entire journey. Probably better than me! We have had so many adventures I can't even think where to begin, so I'll save them for another letter.

Oh, Jenny, I miss you and wish you were here now to share the sights. I miss Alexandria and our house, too, but there is no sense in grieving about it. I hope we'll soon have a settled life. I'll write again when I have an address where you can write back!

Your best friend still, I hope,
Suzannah

Suzannah reread her letter. Just seeing Joad's name made her clench her teeth. His very last words to her and Daniel before they left on the ferry had been, "I'll get ye yet . . . and yer whole high 'n' mighty family!"

Thinking now about his threat, she remembered what Daniel had said: "The Mouts are coming on to St. Louis tomorrow, but they won't know where we're staying. Anyhow, I don't see how he could harm us unless—"

"Unless what?" she had asked.

Daniel drew a pained breath. "Unless it has something to do with Charles."

"I'm not going to think about it," she had said, and pushed the whole idea out of her mind.

She put the letter in her traveling bag and slipped the strings of the bag over her shoulder. Best to mail Jenny's letter before they left for Independence in the morning.

Stepping into the parlor of their hotel suite, Suzannah saw that Pauline was sketching the river scene outside their window, and Charles was lounging on the settee, his feet propped on the coffee table.

He smiled at Suzannah. "You do keep a tight grip on that bag of yours. Don't tell me it's full of money."

A thousand answers flew to mind, but no words came from her mouth.

"Is it?" he asked.

"Is it what?"

"Is it full of money?" he repeated.

"Oh, Charles!" she finally managed, then went to the closet for her cloak. "Wherever would I get money?" Trying to appear composed, she added, "I'm going out for a walk . . . with Daniel."

Charles's hooded eyes followed her every movement. Suzannah fumbled with her cloak, then quickly got it on over her dress and traveling bag. Her conscience pained her. The truth was that she hadn't made arrangements to go walking with Daniel.

"Most young ladies carry their traveling bags outside their cloaks, don't they?" Charles asked smoothly.

"Uncle Franklin said we're to be careful of thieves in St. Louis," she replied. As the words came out, it occurred to her that she was talking to the biggest thief of all. Charles had stolen the family house and furnishings right out from under them!

He removed his feet from the coffee table and rose with a polished grace. "I could do with a little fresh air myself," he said. "Maybe I'll go along with you and Daniel. No sense in both Pauline and me waiting here while Jamie naps."

"You're not taking me gambling with you!" Suzannah objected.

Pauline tucked back a wisp of hair. "Please, Suzannah," she said, "let's not have any trouble."

Suzannah swallowed hard, then went to the door of the room Daniel shared with his father and knocked.

No one answered.

Charles gave a short laugh. "They went out an hour ago. They thought you were resting. Looks as if you're stuck with me after all."

Suzannah managed a smile. "I'll just go down and see if they're waiting in the lobby."

Charles took his topcoat from the closet. "You wait for me, young lady," he said, his tone threatening. "You and your sister are still under my authority."

Suzannah stood very still, afraid she would lose her temper. Pauline continued her sketching, acting as if she had heard nothing. She didn't even speak as they left the room.

Downstairs in the wood-paneled lobby, Charles said, "No sign of Daniel, is there?"

Suzannah shook her head. "No, I don't see him."

"Well, then, the two of us shall take in the sights," he said. "What did you have in mind to see?"

The post office, she thought, but admitting that would be the last thing in the world she would do. He wouldn't be at all pleased that she was writing Jenny in Alexandria. "Whatever is of interest to you," she said in her most polite tone of voice.

"There's plenty of that," he answered agreeably.

They went out to the street and, to Suzannah's amazement, found Joad Mout loitering at the hotel door.

"Well, well," Charles said. "Don't tell me you and your father are staying *here.*"

Joad shot him a hateful look and sauntered off.

"Doesn't say much, does he?" Charles watched him cross the street, then took Suzannah's arm to assist her over a puddle on the sidewalk.

"He made a lot of trouble for his cousin Timmy on the trip," Suzannah said. "He tried to steal Mrs. Fortran's brooch too. He said he's going to get—"

"Ah," Charles said, tipping his hat politely to a man dressed like a showboat gambler. "Joad is doubtless one of those thieves your uncle warned you about."

She decided not to argue. "Probably."

"Now for the grand tour," Charles said. "I've been here long enough to know my way around what's called the Gateway to the West." He imitated a guide's tone. "We stand here at the confluence of the Mississippi and Missouri Rivers, where the waterways are as busy as the streets—"

He was right about that at least. The rivers were as crowded with boats as yesterday. Steamboats chugged downriver, and barges hauled coal and grain. The streets were filled with carriages, buggies, drays, oxcarts, and covered wagons, and the sidewalks teemed with the same sort of colorful people she had described in her letter to— *Jenny's letter!*

How could she mail it now? Likely she'd never have a chance to mail it from Independence. Her mind churned on the problem, but no answer came.

At length, they wandered past the two-story brick house where William Clark, the famous Northwest explorer, had lived.

"William Clark and Meriwether Lewis opened the road to Oregon, as your Meriwether middle-named uncle and cousin have no doubt informed you," Charles said.

110

Suzannah nodded. Apparently he didn't think too highly of Uncle Franklin or Daniel. Probably jealous.

His mood changed abruptly. In fact he looked most pleased. "Tonight I have made plans for the entire family to dine at a fine restaurant. And since there's a splendid bathing room downstairs in our hotel, I made appointments for each of us to have a bath in preparation for the evening."

Now that was something to look forward to! Suzannah hadn't had a proper bath since they'd left home. For the rest of the afternoon, she listened to Charles's lectures without wishing she were somewhere else. Maybe Pauline was right. Maybe Charles Herrington wasn't all bad after all.

It wasn't until Suzannah had dressed for dinner in her best blue dress that she realized someone had been through her things. She rushed to the bed and felt between the mattresses. Missing! Her pouch with the gold coins was missing! She had hidden it there while bathing in the hotel bathing room—

Charles! So that's why he had arranged the bath appointments! How could she have believed, even for a moment, that he could be trusted? For the first time, she felt as disgusted with herself as she was with Pauline.

She rushed out to the parlor and was glad to find Daniel with Pauline and Jamie. Best of all, he was in his old clothes, not yet dressed for dinner. "Who's bathing now?" she asked.

"Charles just went down," Pauline replied, looking especially pretty in a blue sprigged dimity that matched her eyes.

"Come on!" Suzannah grabbed Daniel's arm, and when he opened his mouth to object, she put a finger to her lips.

When they were on their way down the back stairs to the bathing room, she explained what Charles had done. "I'm sure he has my gold coins with him now, so no one can rob him while *he's* in the tub."

"What are we going to do about it?" Daniel asked.

"Do you have your slingshot, string, and fishhooks in your pocket?"

"Sure, just like always."

She grinned. "We're going fishing."

"Fishing?"

"Fishing for my gold coins. I'll tell you about them later. First we'll have to get the bathing door open. I noticed the key bolt doesn't close all the way. Probably because the dampness has swollen the wood."

When they arrived at the bathing room, the "occupied" sign hung from the white porcelain doorknob. Charles, not surprisingly, was singing an Italian opera in the tub, this time *The Barber of Seville*. Even more helpful, pots and pans clanged in the hotel's nearby kitchen.

She tried the doorknob, but it was locked. "A thin coin please," she whispered to Daniel.

He took one from his pocket.

While Charles's loud "Figaro! Figaro! Figaro!" rolled through the air, Suzannah slipped the coin in by the lock, slowly easing it open. "Now the slingshot, string, and fish-hook."

Daniel obliged. It took only a moment longer to tie the fishhook to the string, and the string to the slingshot.

Suzannah put a finger to her lips once more, then opened the door slightly. Charles was fully submerged in the high white porcelain tub, his new clothes carefully folded over a stool. As he scrubbed, he sang lustily, no doubt relieved to have *her* money.

Daniel pointed to himself, hoping to do the deed. But Suzannah shook her head. This was one fishing expedition she'd go on herself.

She opened the door wider, then took dead aim at Charles's clothes with the slingshot. Letting go, she shot and hooked the fabric. Slowly she pulled on the string and, while Charles sang on in his phony Italian, Suzannah reeled out his fine trousers.

Going through the pockets quickly, she found what she was looking for. Sure enough, there was her pouch with the gold coins still inside. She held back a victory whoop while Daniel eased the door shut.

"What'll we do with the trousers?" he whispered, his freckles dancing with mischief.

"Hang 'em on the doorknob on this side," she said.

They had scarcely finished when the singing stopped. There was a deadly silence before Charles bellowed, "My trousers! Someone's stolen my trousers!"

Suzannah raced for the back stairs with Daniel, muffling her laughter. Running up the stairway, she doubled up, laughing so hard her stomach began to hurt.

"I wouldn't have . . . missed that . . . for the world," Daniel gasped out between fits of hysterics.

Suzannah moaned, clutching her stomach. "Afraid I'll remember it every time Charles sings one of his infernal operas!"

As they went on to their rooms, Daniel said, "The best thing about it is that Charles can't complain to anyone about being robbed of what's not his!"

"It's going to be hard keeping a straight face when we see him at dinner, but I guess we'd better not give ourselves away."

Promising to keep their secret, they entered the hotel parlor as solemn as if they were going to church. Suzannah hurried through to her bedroom, locking the door behind her. No more baths, unless she took the coins right into the tub with her, she vowed.

She was just returning the coin pouch to her traveling bag when she realized that something else was missing: *Oh, no! Jenny's letter!*

Charles must have taken that too!

CHAPTER 11

The next morning, they boarded a squat, snub-nosed Missouri River steamboat with twin smokestacks that rose like rabbit's ears on each side of the wheelhouse. Today they would be heading for Independence, the end of the journey. At last they'd be able to settle down again and start a new life, Suzannah thought.

The boat gave a throaty blast of its horn. As they chugged away, smoke from the two smokestacks engulfed them, and the coughing passengers hurried to the other side of the deck.

"This is no showboat," Charles remarked glumly.

Suzannah both ignored and avoided him—as she had ever since retrieving her gold coins the night before. She wished for Daniel, but he was resting in his cabin, not feeling well.

Once the smoke had trailed off into the air, they stood with the other passengers and watched the city of St. Louis disappear behind them. After a while Suzannah strolled along the deck, getting used to the feel of the boat's movement beneath her feet.

At length Charles joined her. "Were you near the hotel bathing room last night when I was in there?"

"What would I be doing there?" she bluffed.

"I thought maybe you'd forgotten something from your bath."

"I didn't forget anything—"

Charles glared at her. "Don't you ever write to anyone in Alexandria again, do you hear?"

If his words had failed to deliver the message, there was no mistaking his tone. She had never disliked anyone so much in her whole life, and now he was trying to frighten her!

"What right do you have to go through my things?" she demanded. "What right—?"

"The right of kin, my dear. You haven't forgotten that you are now a member of *my* household, have you?"

Suzannah felt her face flush with anger, and she walked to the ship's rail before Charles could say any more. Why, oh why had Pauline ever married him? She stared blindly out at the wake of the ship.

From midship she heard Pauline calling to her. "Suzannah, you'll be black with smoke. Why don't you come over here with me?"

Suzannah sighed and turned dutifully, finding her sister sitting in a deck chair, attempting a riverside sketch of St. Louis. Suzannah sat down beside her.

"Charles has his faults," Pauline began, keeping her eyes on her work, "but I do wish the two of you got along better."

Suzannah's heart sank. "I wish we did too," she said in a small voice. All the anger and resentment she felt for Charles mingled now with guilt. Why *couldn't* she get along with him, if only for Pauline's sake?

"Then please forgive him," her sister said, looking up from her sketching. "I don't believe God wants us to keep score of the wrongs done against us, do you? Being unforgiving just makes us unhappy. The Bible says when someone strikes us, we're to turn the other cheek."

Suzannah gave Pauline a sidelong look. Maybe her sister wasn't the coward she'd supposed her to be. Maybe she had truly learned how to forgive.

She was right about something else too. Suzannah knew she hadn't forgiven Charles for selling their house out from under them. And she certainly hadn't forgiven him for abandoning Pauline and Jamie to ride on ahead to gamble away everything else they had. And neither had she forgiven him for marrying Pauline in the first place and making all their lives so wretched.

"Have *you* forgiven him?" she asked Pauline.

"Yes. I have."

"I don't see how you can do that!" Suzannah blurted.

"I can't do it alone," her sister admitted. "But whether I want to or not, I have to say, 'Lord, I want to forgive. Help me. Give me Thy love for him.' "

Suzannah's shoulders drooped. "I don't know if I even *want* to forgive him."

"Then that's something you'll have to take to the Lord," Pauline said quietly, turning to her drawing pad.

Suzannah got up and walked to the opposite rail. How could she forgive Charles when he'd ruined their lives? How could God even expect it? It was just too much to ask.

Gazing at the muddy waters of the Missouri, surrounded by green forested banks, Suzannah saw a flatboat with a family aboard, the father poling. She felt a tug of envy. How she wished that were her own family, that Papa and Mama were still alive.

She caught a glimpse of Daniel standing with Charles and Uncle Franklin near the stern of the boat. She was glad to see that her cousin was feeling better, but she'd wait until she could catch him alone. Meanwhile, he seemed interested in the men's conversation.

"Yes," said one of the passengers, "the Missouri is crookeder, muddier, shallower, and has swifter currents than any other river. Not to mention snags, sandbars, and a wind that'll blow a boat right out of the channel! Got to tie up at night, you know."

"No one told me we tied up at night!" Charles sputtered.

Uncle Franklin replied, "I fear I'm at fault for not informing you, Charles, but the ticket agent did tell me."

So Charles hadn't even bought their tickets! Suzannah fumed, madder than ever. Most likely, he had already gambled away every cent of their house money.

The cabins of the riverboat were as dirty as the twisting, muddy river. But with the weather turning cold and rainy, Suzannah stayed inside with Pauline and Jamie for most of the three-day trip to Independence.

On the third evening, she was relieved to see the dock at the wooded Wayne City Landing. At least the trip on the dirty steamboat was over and soon she wouldn't have to share such close quarters with her brother-in-law.

Uncle Franklin hired a buggy at the landing. But even the beauty of the forests on the ride to Independence didn't help

Suzannah change her frame of mind. If anything, she was even more angry and depressed.

When they rolled into town, Suzannah found that Independence, crowded with shanties and log buildings, was much smaller than St. Louis, and even noisier. Tawdry signs lined the dirt streets: "Goods for Santa Fe trade! Goods for Oregon and California! All new, all cheap!"

Seeing Suzannah's dismay, Uncle Franklin patted her hand. "I expect it will be quieter at Aunt Pearl's. She lives in the country, you know."

Never during the entire journey had she wanted to go home to Alexandria more than she did right now. What if Aunt Pearl didn't want her, or Pauline and her family? Aunt Pearl wasn't even a Colton.

"Tell me again about Aunt Pearl," Suzannah asked Pauline, who was sitting beside her.

"Well, she's Aunt Ruthie's youngest sister, of course. And you already know that her husband and two children died last summer of the fevers, and she's all alone now."

Turning to Aunt Ruthie, Suzannah persisted. "I know Aunt Pearl invited you and your family to visit. But what if she doesn't want the rest of us?"

Aunt Ruthie gave a laugh. "Knowing Pearl, she'll only say, 'The more, the merrier.'"

Suzannah hoped it was true. But if not, she'd just have to use her gold coins to take them back to Alexandria . . . or even to buy a place to live here.

It was nearly sunset when the hired buggy turned up the wooded drive to Aunt Pearl's house on the hillside.

"Why, it's a log house!" Aunt Ruthie exclaimed. "How charming!"

Suzannah sent up a fervent prayer. *Please, Lord, let everything work out!*

When the buggy came to a stop in front of the house, a blond woman appeared on the porch to greet them.

"Why, she looks just like Mother!" Daniel said.

Aunt Ruthie laughed as she climbed out of the buggy. "Only a lot younger and thinner!"

"Ruthie!" Aunt Pearl called out. "Oh, Ruthie, it's been so long!"

In moments they were in each other's arms, and Suzannah's worries about Aunt Pearl began to melt away. She might be a widow in her thirties, but she was quick as a girl, and just as pretty.

Suzannah felt even better when Aunt Pearl welcomed her with a twinkle in her eye. "I'm especially pleased to meet you, Suzannah. Ruthie wrote what close cousins you and Daniel are. What a shame if you'd been separated."

"I guess so," Suzannah replied, trying to ignore the face Daniel was making at her. She'd give him a proper poke later. "It's nice to meet you, too . . . even nicer than I thought—I mean—"

Aunt Pearl laughed and hugged her, then lifted Jamie into her arms. "As for you, Jamie Herrington, I plan to spoil you as much as your mama will allow." And as they started for the house, she beamed at all of them. "What a joy to have you here at last."

Maybe things would turn out fine after all, Suzannah hoped. Nonetheless, she kept her drawstring traveling bag with the gold coins tucked under her arm.

At breakfast the next morning, they all sat at Aunt Pearl's table, devouring eggs, bacon, and light-as-air flapjacks drenched in golden butter.

"I do love Sundays," Aunt Pearl said. "I can't wait to introduce all of you to my friends at church."

Suzannah saw Charles frown, but to her amazement, Pauline said, "Charles and I are eager to go."

Charles blinked with shock, then saw everyone watching him. He finally managed a small smile and a nod.

He probably didn't want to make trouble with Aunt Pearl right away, Suzannah thought. Then she prayed, *Lord, soften Charles's hard heart this morning. No one else can change him!*

"We won't all fit in the buggy," Aunt Pearl said, "so I propose we ride in the new wagon. There are benches, so there will be plenty of seats. I'm sure it's not what you were used to in Georgetown and Alexandria, but here on the frontier, we're not quite so elegant."

"Perhaps Pauline and I could—" Charles began.

But Uncle Franklin cut him off. "All of us riding in the wagon together would be fairest, Charles."

Suzannah glanced at Charles again. At least he was trying to look agreeable.

After breakfast they dressed in their Sunday clothes and hurried out to the new wagon.

"Charles, would you take the reins? You look like a man who knows horses," Aunt Pearl suggested.

"I do," replied Charles with a careless smile, "but only those one rides."

"Then you'll learn something new this morning," Aunt Pearl replied, undaunted.

Suzannah and Daniel grinned at each other.

At length, they arrived at the small white church with its simple steeple. Charles hitched the horses while the rest of them started for the church door.

Inside, soft organ music filled the white sanctuary, and Suzannah sat down on an oak pew between Pauline and Daniel. Her program said, *Commit thy way unto the Lord; trust also in him; and he shall bring it to pass. Psalm 37:5.* It sure was hard to commit oneself to the Lord when one had an independent streak, she thought miserably.

Daniel had found the page in the hymnal and was sharing it with her as he sang out in his fine voice:

O worship the King, all glorious above,
And gratefully sing His power and His love:
Our Shield and Defender, the Ancient of Days,
Pavilioned in splendor, and girded with praise.

Suzannah sang on about God's might and His grace. They sang the last verse, and the words thundered in her heart— "His mercies how tender, how firm to the end, our Maker, Defender, Redeemer, and Friend."

"His mercies . . ." That meant God's *forgiveness*. He had sure forgiven her many times. To Suzannah's surprise, the pastor had more to say on the subject.

"Like God, we must be merciful," he said. "If you do not forgive others, no matter what they do, your heart will harden with bitterness."

Suzannah drew a deep breath. Deep down inside, she had to admit she felt plenty bitter about Charles. The more she thought about it, the more she realized how much her bitterness had controlled her life. She was always thinking up ways to avoid Charles, and when they were together, she was either mad or trying to think up some scheme to get back at him for all the misery he had caused.

The pastor must have been reading her thoughts, for he said, "Little minds fill with anger and revenge. They don't know the pleasure of forgiving one's enemies. Forgiveness is the proper work of a Christian's heart."

As she listened, it was as if the Lord Himself were speaking, telling her in a still, small voice just what to do. It was not enough that she put up with Charles. She must give up the bitterness toward him just as she had given up trying to control Timmy's life. She must give her bitterness to God. *Lord*, she prayed, *help me! Take away this bitterness about Charles and help me to forgive him. Give me Thy love for him.*

Slowly, slowly her heart began to soften, then to fill with love—love not only for those who already loved her, but for all people, for Charles too!

I thank Thee, Lord, she prayed joyously. *It seemed so impossible. Oh, I thank Thee!*

All the way home, love and joy so overflowed her heart that the earth seemed a most beautiful sight. Suzannah scarcely heard the lively conversation in the wagon except when Uncle Franklin said, "The sermon was a good reminder to me to trust the Lord more and more."

When they arrived at Aunt Pearl's log house, however, three rough-looking men were waiting on their front porch, their horses tethered nearby.

Charles stopped the wagon abruptly and started to jump, ready to run. Before he was halfway down, they grabbed him by the collar of his Sunday suit.

"This time, you pay up, Herrington," said one of the ruffians. "We've followed you all the way from Virginia to collect our money."

Suzannah sat frozen in the wagon. She recognized him . . . the hawk-nosed man who had stopped their carriage the night they had left Alexandria.

Charles sputtered, then turned his fury on Suzannah. "It's *your* fault . . . you and your letters! They've traced me through—"

The hawk-nosed man jerked Charles back. "Weren't no letters. Only help we had was from a boy named Joad, but we could've found you without any help from him or anybody else. Now, pay up! You owe us the proceeds from yer Alexandria house."

"But I don't have the money—"

The biggest man drew up a gun and stuck it in Charles's back. "Then you better git it. We aim to have that money . . . or yer life."

The words hung in the air around them, and Suzannah knew the man meant what he said. It was either the money . . . or they would kill Charles. Pauline wouldn't have a husband and Jamie wouldn't have a father. Somebody had to do something.

Lord, help! Tell me what to do!

"My luck turned bad in St. Louis!" Charles protested. "If you'll give me time—"

"Your time has just run out," said one of the others. "You ain't to be trusted. You promised again 'n' again."

The still, small voice in Suzannah's heart urged, *Do it . . . save his life . . . Don't hang on to your gold or to your own way.*

124

She held back, but the still, small voice came again: *Trust Me, Suzannah.*

In a flash, she recalled Uncle Franklin's explanation of Charles's gambling. He'd gotten trapped just like people get trapped by any sin. Just like *she'd* been trapped by her own stubborn desire to run her own life. She considered how much she loved Pauline and Jamie, and remembered what Uncle Franklin had said about trusting the Lord more and more.

The words from Mother's favorite Psalm came to her again: *Yea, though I walk through the valley of the shadow of death, I will fear no evil: for thou art with me.* That meant He would be with her in trouble, too.

She rose and took a step forward in the wagon as if someone had pushed her. "I—I have some gold coins," she said, taking the traveling bag from her shoulder. "I hope it's . . . enough."

She opened the drawstrings of the bag and took out the coin pouch. Everyone gasped when they saw the gold. "Father gave these to me just before . . . he and Mother died. I—I've been trusting too much in them . . . instead of in God. I want to give them in exchange for Charles's life."

Leaning down from the wagon, Suzannah poured out the gold coins into the big man's hands before she could change her mind. Then she heard herself saying, "I'm sure this is what Father would have wanted me to do."

Uncle Franklin cleared his throat. "I do believe he would."

"It don't cover it, girl," the hawk-nosed man said, "but it'll do."

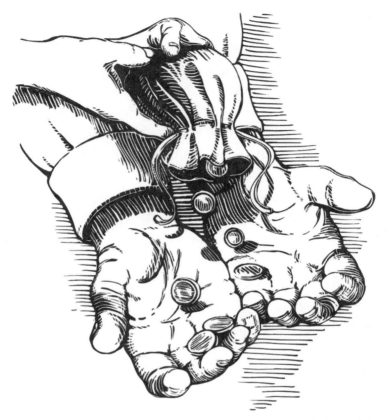

With that, the third man grabbed Charles and threw him to the ground. "A wonder you hadn't stole 'em from her already."

"He tried," Daniel spoke up, "but we got them back!"

Suzannah shot him a warning look, but the men just mounted their horses and rode away down the drive without so much as a backward glance.

Charles picked himself up off the ground and brushed the dust off his fine trousers. "I suppose you think you bought me now."

His ingratitude shocked Suzannah at first. Then she shook her head as she climbed down from the wagon. "No . . . I never thought that. I only know it's what the Lord wanted me to do."

Pauline hugged her, tears streaming down her face. "Oh, Suzannah, I'm so grateful! I can never thank you enough—"

Then the rest of the family was gathering around to give her hugs and congratulations. But before they could get a word in, she spoke up. "I didn't do anything. It was the Lord's work. Besides, most of you know what the real Suzannah Elizabeth Colton is like. She would never have done a thing like that!"

Daniel grinned, then tugged one of her braids. "That's for sure! Suzannah Elizabeth Colton didn't do it!"

She aimed a poke at him, but he dodged and ran. She took off after him, throwing down the traveling bag and suddenly feeling free of a terrible burden.

As she ran after her cousin, Suzannah felt as if her feet had wings. She'd never have to worry about the coins again. She wouldn't need them for courage either. Not when she had the Lord, who had helped her through a carriage chase, a blizzard, a bear chase, a runaway Conestoga wagon, meeting a trapper who was touched in the head . . . and far more. The Lord was her strength. And strangest of all, she had learned to depend on Him in a place called Independence!

As she chased Daniel toward the back of the log house, she heard Uncle Franklin say, "Those kids! Those Colton cousins!"

She guessed he was shaking his head and grinning like Father once had . . . like a Colton should. And she wondered if Father and Mother up in heaven would somehow know and be pleased.

EPILOGUE

The next day at breakfast, Aunt Pearl spilled maple syrup on the kitchen floor, then a dish of gravy before dinner. And all afternoon, she seemed nervous, watching the front windows as if she were expecting someone.

"Whatever's wrong, Pearl?" asked Aunt Ruthie. "You're as nervous as a cat with a new litter of kittens. Is it something about the last letter you wrote?"

Aunt Pearl nodded. "It is." Her blue eyes widened as two riders galloped up the road to the log house. "And now's the time to tell you, too, because here come Karl and Garth. The fact is . . . I got married a month ago."

"Married! You got married without telling me, your only sister?" Aunt Ruthie seemed hurt.

"I'm sorry, Ruthie. But I was so lonely . . . so I just up and said yes when out of the blue, Karl Stengler proposed. You'll meet him . . . and his fourteen-year-old son, Garth. They've been in St. Louis this week, telling some of his family there good-bye."

"Good-bye?" Uncle Franklin asked. "I thought you had been married for a month—"

"Excuse me!" Aunt Pearl interrupted, tucking in loose strands of blond hair as she rushed for the door. "I'll let them know you're here."

Suzannah watched through the parlor window as the three of them spoke earnestly.

Finally they came into the house with Aunt Pearl. In the parlor, she smiled anxiously. Suzannah suspected that her aunt was hoping her family would approve of her decision.

"This is Karl Stengler, my new husband," she introduced the tall, dark-haired man. "And this is my new son, Garth."

"Pleased to meet you," Karl said stiffly, shaking hands with Charles and Uncle Franklin. He was dark as an Indian, and so bony that his Adam's apple bobbed noticeably when he spoke.

Garth stared at her from under the same heavy dark brows as Karl. "Pleased to meet you," he said, looking even less pleased than his father. He kept his hands to himself.

"Well," Aunt Pearl began, "why don't we all sit down and get acquainted?"

"We'll wait on that, Pearl," Karl Stengler said shortly. "We have the horses to see to." Then he turned to his guests. "Pearl wrote to warn you, but she said you didn't get the letter, and she ain't had the heart to tell you yet." He looked at his new wife. "Unless you do it now, I will."

"Tell us? Tell us what?" asked Daniel and Aunt Ruthie at the very same time.

Suzannah cringed, fearing the worst. *Now what?*

Aunt Pearl said, "Well . . . with me losing my family and all, and Karl's wife dead, too . . . well, we wanted to make a new life for ourselves . . . away from Missouri. The fact is, we've sold our farms, and we're leaving in two weeks for the Oregon Territory."

"Oregon?" they all said.

Aunt Pearl nodded. "We hoped you might change your minds about opening a trading post and go with us in the covered wagon train."

"There's good free land for farmin'," Karl Stengler said.

Suzannah glanced at Daniel. His eyes were as big as saucers, and even his freckles had faded.

But Uncle Franklin was smiling. "I've always dreamed of going there . . . but I don't know—"

Just when we thought we were settling down! Suzannah thought. *And now maybe Oregon! I need Thee, Lord, more than ever.*